THE CASE OF THE BROWN SCRAGGLY DOG

I0662750

(DAVEY & DEREK JUNIOR DETECTIVES SERIES, BOOK 4)

JANICE SPINA

Copyright 2016

By Janice Spina
All rights reserved

DEDICATION

To my two middle grandsons, Jason and Joey, who love to read about mysteries and adventures and inspire me to write more

ACKNOWLEDGEMENTS

Thank you to my beta readers, John Spina and Michele Rolfe, for their tireless efforts to read and review this book and for their helpful input.

OTHER BOOKS BY JANICE SPINA:

Pre-School to Grade Three:

Louey the Lazy Elephant
Ricky the Rambunctious Raccoon

Jerry the Crabby Crayfish
Lamby the Lonely Lamb
*(*Received Silver Medal from
Mom's Choice Awards)

Jesse the Precocious Polar Bear
Broose the Moose on the Loose
Sebastian Meets Marvin the
Monkey

Middle-Grade/Preteen:

Davey & Derek Junior Detectives
Book 1
The Case of the Missing Cell Phone
(Won Pinnacle Book Achievement
Award & Readers' Favorite Award –
Honorable Mention)

The Case of the Mysterious Black
Cat (Won Pinnacle Book

Achievement Award) (*Davey & Derek Junior Detectives Series Book 2)*

The Case of the Magical Ivory Elephant (Davey & Derek Junior Detectives Series Book 3)

Novels: (under J.E. Spina)

Hunting Mariah

How Far Is Heaven

Table of Contents

INTRODUCTION

Davey and Derek Donato are twins but not identical. They each have their own distinct talents and are junior detectives by their own design. They live in the quiet town of Lindon, New Hampshire where nothing much happens, reason why the boys look for adventures.

They gleaned the idea to be detectives from a book their parents bought each of them for their tenth birthday on July 15th.

Davey, with black hair and green eyes, is the older twin by three minutes and teases his brother all the time about being the baby brother. He is an intellectual and quite patient and observant. Davey has an incredible skill where anything he reads can be committed to memory. This is extremely helpful when he has to help Derek who hasn't done the required reading for school ahead of time. Davey also likes to take things apart in order to find out how they work.

Derek, with light brown hair and green eyes, on the other hand, is a thinker and somewhat of a dreamer. He thinks things through and likes to be in control and see things running smoothly. He excels in writing, math and problem solving. He does have an aptitude for getting into all kinds of trouble by himself. Trouble, unfortunately, seems to follow him, but luckily Davey always backs Derek up.

The boys also have a friend, Mickey Catonni, aka Cat, with wiry red hair, who helped the boys in their first case, *The Case of the Missing Cell Phone.* Mickey is a cool kind of kid who knows how to communicate by signing. He has a fun personality, great sense of humor and gets along well with others.

Mickey has a little sister, Jenny, who is deaf. Knowing sign language helps Mickey to talk with Jenny. Jenny plays an important part in *Book 2, The Case of the Mysterious Black Cat.*

There are more magical adventures in *Book 3, The Case of the Magical Ivory Elephant* where the unexpected happens to Davey and Derek.

THE CASE OF THE BROWN SCRAGGLY DOG

(DAVEY & DEREK JR. SERIES DETECTIVES BOOK 4)

Written by Janice Spina

Illustrations and Cover by John Spina

Published by Janice Spina 2016

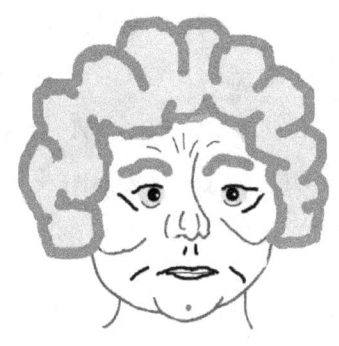

CHAPTER ONE

A Steely Gaze

The twins rushed over to Great Aunt Gigi's house to continue honing their magical skills under her expert tutelage. They had so far learned one magic trick just before they completed their third case with the magical ivory elephant named Tamba.

Today Aunt Gigi had promised to begin training them with their wands to perform other simple incantations. Davey raced on ahead of his brother, Derek, and arrived at Aunt Gigi's door first much to Derek's dismay.

"Why won't you let me beat you just once, Davey? You cheated anyway. You jumped on your bike before I got mine out of the garage. That's not fair!"

"Oh, all right Derek. It was a tie, okay?" Davey stated as he smirked his way up their aunt's stairs.

"I see your face, Davey. It's not funny. I will beat you fair and square one day. Just you wait, Bro!" Derek threatened as he followed behind mumbling to himself.

Aunt Gigi was at the door and heard the interchange between the boys. She feared that this was not a good time to have them use their powers. They were clearly upset with one another. That could be dangerous.

Davey rang Aunt Gigi's doorbell and waited next to his disgruntled brother as Aunt Gigi opened the door and welcomed them in.

Both boys nodded and said, 'Hi Aunt Gigi,' and artfully ducked under her outstretched arms. Aunt Gigi was getting used to their tactics to avoid her bone-crushing hugs and laughed good-naturedly.

"So what's new boys?" Aunt Gigi watched the twins' faces for any sign of trouble brewing.

"Oh, nothing much, Aunt Gigi. We wanted…um…we wanted to ask if you could teach us some more magic. You did say to come back on Monday," Derek ventured forward.

"Well, I guess I did. Hmm, is it Monday already?" Aunt Gigi smiled broadly with amusement.

Davey and Derek swapped surprised looks as they used "TT" (twin telepathy) to share their exasperation over their aunt's teasing.

"Oh, sorry boys, I'm just kidding you. I know it's Monday. Besides, I have been waiting patiently for you to come over. I thought you would never get here." Aunt Gigi's smile grew wider.

"Well, sorry we're so late, Aunt Gigi. But Mom, before she left for work, had us cleaning our already clean rooms for the third time since Saturday," Davey exclaimed more than a little peeved.

"I wish we could just use our wands to clean up our rooms, Aunt Gigi. Can you teach us how to do that?" Davey dared to ask such a question.

Derek looked shocked at his brother for his bravado or stupidity more likely for saying this.

Aunt Gigi turned her gaze toward Davey as her eyes grew larger with fiery sparks appearing.

Davey jumped back in alarm and closed his eyes to avoid looking at this frightening display of anger.

Derek grabbed hold of his brother and pulled him back away from Aunt Gigi in case she decided to use her magic on him and change him into a pig or something worse.

Davey choked out the words, "I'm...I'm sorry, Aunt Gigi. I didn't mean to say that. I really don't want to know how to do that. I don't mind cleaning my room, really!"

Aunt Gigi's fiery expression changed back to her sweet, old lady one which she used most of the time. It now seemed unsettling to look at for the boys, because now they knew what she was capable of when angry.

"Yeah, Aunt Gigi, Davey didn't mean anything. He is kind of lazy at times."

Using "TT" the boys said, *oh, my God, did you see her eyes, Davey?*

Of course, I did you ninny. She was looking at me after all! I never want to see that expression on her face again. I thought she was going to burn me up!

Yeah, so did I, Bro. You better be more careful from now on. She has much more power than we do.

The boys stopped sharing thoughts and looked serious and contrite as they again expressed their apologies for this mistake together.

"So sorry, Aunt Gigi. Do you forgive us, or Davey, I mean?"

"Yes, of course, my boys. I know you were only kidding and wouldn't want to ever do that. Now are you ready to begin more training?" Aunt Gigi smiled benignly and turned to pick up her magic box.

"Boys, before we begin I made you some snacks. Let's go out into the kitchen and have some."

The boys were not really hungry but when they spied the table full of dips, veggies and healthy whole wheat chips they dug in.

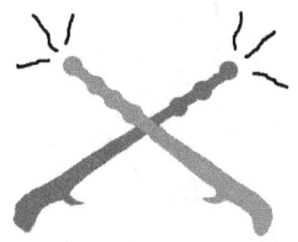

CHAPTER TWO

Fun with Magic

Wands were flying around as Davey and Derek followed their aunt's instructions explicitly. They now tried to do the incantation all by themselves.

"Boys, concentrate on the words you have to say and keep your wand up and parallel to your body swinging it in a figure eight. Good, nicely done," Aunt Gigi smiled proudly as the twins picked up quickly on her teachings.

The figurine of a black panther disappeared from the shelf and soon appeared in a different place in front of the boys much to their surprise and delight.

"Wow, did you see that, Davey? The panther disappeared and came back where we commanded."

"That is way cool, Derek. I can't believe we did it! Thank you, Aunt Gigi!"

"You are doing well, Derek and Davey. I'm proud of you both. It looks like you have that trick down pat. Now let's try something fun, shall we?" Aunt Gigi giggled in anticipation.

"Yes, we're ready!" the boys eagerly answered.

"Okay, please walk to the middle of the room and hold your wands out in front of you as far as you can. Point toward the wall to the photo of Uncle George and me in our garden. Say, "ekat su yawa ot eht nedrag.""

The boys repeated the backwards words in the sentence and disappeared from the room ending up in the garden.

"Davey, look where we are! I can't believe we left the room! Where is Aunt Gigi?"

The boys could hear someone laughing but couldn't see anyone around. Right in front of their eyes popped up Aunt Gigi with a wide grin on her crinkled face.

"Ha ha boys, you looked so surprised that you did it! Great job! I was right behind you. No worries. I will always be close by to make sure you are safe."

"Oh, Aunt Gigi. You made me jump!" Derek said clearly startled.

"Are you okay, Derek?" Davey was shaking too from the surprise but recovered quicker.

"Yeah, Bro, I'm okay. I can't believe we can do magic! This is too much to believe!"

"I know, Derek. We are magicians, or maybe more than just magicians," Davey proudly exclaimed.

"Well, you could say that, boys. You are definitely becoming more than magicians. You will soon be talented young warlocks. But there is much more to teach you."

"Okay, we're ready," Davey declared.

Out of the corner of his eyes, Derek, suddenly saw a brown blur run by the garden where they were standing.

Using "TT" Derek asked, *did you see that, Davey? There's something out there just beyond the garden.*

Yes, I saw it too. Let's go explore and see what it is.

"What's wrong boys? Did you see something?"

"Yes, Aunt Gigi. There's something out there in the woods."

"Well, let's go see what it is, why don't we?"

The three of them walked forward slowly with stealth to the tree line and peeked into the high grass.

CHAPTER THREE

A Brown Scraggly Dog

Cowering in the grass was a large brown scraggly dog with frightened eyes. The dog warily looked up at the boys and their aunt.

Davey moved toward the dog and put out his hand for the dog to sniff.

Curiosity got the better of the dog as he ventured out of the grass to get a closer look and sniff of these humans.

"Hey boy, what are you doing here? Where did you come from?" Davey bent down to talk to the dog.

"Derek, look, there's something on the dog's front paw."

"Yeah, I see it. What is it?"

Aunt Gigi moved in to take a closer look too. The smile on her face disappeared as she examined the paw.

"What is it, Aunt Gigi?" Derek probed.

Aunt Gigi leaned in next to the dog and whispered into his ear. The dog's ears perked up and he jumped up and ran away.

"Is he injured? What happened to him, Aunt Gigi? Where's he going?" Davey queried.

"What did you say to him, Aunt Gigi?" Derek questioned further.

"No, he is fine. He's going home. I'll find him; don't worry boys. Let's go in and check with Mianna (Aunt Gigi's cat's spirit that lives in her crystal ball). Maybe she can tell us something about this dog. Take my hands and hold on tight. We're going for a short trip."

In a split second the three were back in the living room still holding onto each other's hands.

"Wow that was fast, Aunt Gigi!" Davey exclaimed.

"It looked like we were going through a swirling tunnel of color! So cool, Aunt Gigi! How did you do that?" Derek shouted.

"With a lot of practice, my dear boy! It takes a lot of practice. You will do all this and more. Be patient and practice will pay off one day for you both," Aunt Gigi stated.

"Come, with me. Let's get my crystal ball. Mianna is waiting there."

"We haven't seen Mianna since our second case. How's she doing?" Davey inquired with a sly smile.

"She's quite well, my boy. Always ready to help when needed," Aunt Gigi smiled back.

She pulled out her magic box and placed the crystal ball on the kitchen table in front of her and the twins. Looking into the ball Aunt Gigi waved her hands over it as she waited for an image to appear.

Looking up at the three was Mianna waving her paw. The cat was clearly upset and gestured wildly to Aunt Gigi. Another image suddenly appeared beside Mianna. It was the brown scraggly dog looking sad.

Aunt Gigi recited some magical words and Mianna nodded and followed the dog as he headed out of their sight.

"What's happening, Aunt Gigi? Where's the dog and Mianna going?" Davey inquired.

"Don't fret, boys. Mianna knows what to do. She'll report back to me what she finds out. It must be time for you two to get on home now. Your mom will be looking for you."

"Huh, oh yeah, okay, Aunt Gigi. Come on, Derek. Let's go."

"But…what about the dog? I want to know what happened to him. Will we see him again?"

"Oh, I think you will, Derek, sooner than you think. Boys, just a minute. Did you enjoy learning another incantation today?"

"Sure did, Aunt Gigi! It was too cool. I can't wait to do more," Davey shouted out as Derek nodded in agreement.

"There'll be plenty more to come. I assure you, dear boys. I enjoyed spending time with you and look forward to the next time." Aunt Gigi put her arms out to get in a quick hug.

The boys were ready for her and ducked under her outstretched arms as they ran for the door yelling, "Bye, Aunt Gigi! See you tomorrow."

Aunt Gigi chuckled and waved as she watched her nephews ride away on their bikes.

Once the boys left Gigi went back to her crystal ball and asked Mianna for the dog's address. Floating up in the ball was 10 Tangerine Lane.

CHAPTER FOUR

A New Case

Davey and Derek raced home excited to share with their mother their time with magic and Aunt Gigi. Also, they had a new case to solve.

"Hey Mom, guess what?" Davey beat his brother back to the garage and parked his bike at the back.

"Davey!!! You cheated again! You never let me win! Hey, did you do something to rev up your bike?"

"Maybe, maybe not," Davey chuckled.

"Hi boys. What's going on? Are you fighting again?"

"No, not really Mom. We have a lot to tell you!" Derek was out of breath from the race home and took a minute to catch his breath to tell his mother the news.

"Come on in boys and tell me everything. Did you have fun today?"

"Wow, you won't believe what we did?" Derek chirped in before Davey could say anything and continued, "We performed another magic trick!"

"Really, that's great! What kind of magic trick?" Laura was anxious to find out.

Davey took over with the explanation in extensive detail. "After we did the trick Aunt Gigi brought us back into the house. It was unreal, Mom! It felt like we were floating through a tunnel with swirling colors."

"That sounds cool! Please be careful, boys, and listen to Aunt Gigi." Laura's face relaxed showing relief that the boys didn't get into trouble.

The boys noticed their mother relax and used "TT" before trying to convince her by saying, "Nothing to worry about, Mom. We're okay. Aunt

Gigi watches us closely when we do magic," Davey stressed.

"Okay, I know she does. I'm just a little wary of all this magic stuff. Just pay attention to your aunt."

"Okay, Mom, will do," the boys agreed.

Laura moved toward the kitchen but was abruptly stopped by Derek's urgent request, "Hey Mom, don't leave yet. We have some more news to share."

Exchanging "TT" once again before continuing, "We have a new case, Mom!"

"Really, what's it about?" Laura asked as her eyes widened in surprise.

Davey explained, "We saw a dog out in Aunt Gigi's yard. He was brown and scraggly-looking. Sure needs a good bath. He looks like he could be a stray."

"I see, so what is the case?"

"The dog, Mom!" Derek stressed.

"Well, you lost me here."

"Oh, yeah, I'll explain," Davey proceeded to give more details about the dog and how Mianna was involved.

"It does look as if you have a new case," Laura nodded in agreement.

"Mianna is going to help us find the dog and where he came from."

"Okay, just don't go wandering around looking for him. You could get into more than you bargained for."

"No problem, Mom. Aunt Gigi will let us know what to do next when Mianna finds him. There was something on his paw but Aunt Gigi wouldn't tell us what it was. I have a feeling it could be blood."

"What? What did you say?"

"I said, it could be blood," Davey recounted.

"Was he hurt?"

"No, Aunt Gigi said he wasn't. So it must be someone else's blood," Derek reported.

"Or maybe it was from an injury that he sustained earlier and is now healed."

"Yeah, I guess that could be it. Aunt Gigi will know soon. We're going back to her house tomorrow. Okay?" Davey questioned.

"Okay, but like I just said, be careful."

"Sure, Mom. We're always careful. Aunt Gigi won't let us get into any trouble. She keeps a close watch over us," Derek chuckled.

"Good. Now is that all you have to report, boys?"

"Oh, yeah. That's it, Mom," Davey said.

"Well, I've got to get dinner ready before your father gets home. Go get cleaned up and you can set the table for me."

"All right, Mom," the twins agreed.

CHAPTER FIVE

Help from Cat

"Hey Derek, let's call Cat. He needs to hear about the dog case."

"Oh, yeah, I bet he'll be excited about a new case. I'll get him on the phone right away." Derek headed out of his brother's room.

"Wait one minute, Derek. What if this dog doesn't have an owner? Do you think that Mom and Dad would let us keep him?"

"Nah, probably not, Bro. I think you're jumping ahead. We don't know anything about this dog. He must have a home. Mianna will be able to tell us soon."

"Yeah, you're probably right, Derek." Davey looked sad as he watched his brother go downstairs to make the call.

Cat's phone rang several times without any answer. Derek ran upstairs to report to his brother. He got as far as the top of the stairs when their phone rang.

Davey leaned out of his room to talk to Derek as their mother called up to report Mickey was on the phone.

44

Derek ran back downstairs to take the call and took the phone from his mother with a, "Thanks Mom."

"Hey Derek. Did you just try to call me?" Cat's excited voice asked.

"Yeah, I did. Have some exciting news for you."

"What? What news?"

Derek began to relay the story of the dog leaving out, of course, any mention of the magic they had performed. Too bad because that was the best part of their day, he thought.

Cat began peppering Derek with questions. "Where did the dog go? How are you going to find him?"

"Aunt Gigi is going to help us...umm. I mean, she said she will keep an eye out for him." Derek's mind raced ahead as he tried not to give any information about Mianna and the help she was giving them from her perch in the crystal ball. This was going to be a tough case if they couldn't share some of this stuff with Cat.

"When are you going back to your aunt's house? Can I go over there to? Maybe we'll see the dog."

"Yeah, let me ask my mom if you can go there. I don't know if Aunt Gigi wants to look after another kid though," Derek answered warily.

"Hey, I'm not a baby, you know, Derek. No one has to look after me." Cat was clearly insulted.

"Sorry, Cat, I didn't mean to say you need a sitter but Aunt Gigi does look after us while Mom is at work. We can come and go home when we need something but we stay around Aunt Gigi's place most of the day until Mom gets home."

"Oh, I don't want to be a bother to her."

"No, I don't think she would mind and besides she makes the best snacks!" Derek proceeded to describe in detail all the snacks that he and Davey had eaten so far there.

"Wow, now I really want to go there. Mom doesn't make snacks like that. When will you know if I can go tomorrow?" Cat was salivating as he spoke.

"Wait a minute, Cat. Let me ask Mom right now. Hold on, okay?"

Cat could hear whispering in the background but couldn't make out what was being said. He waited anxiously until he heard Derek's voice.

"Well, what did she say, Derek?"

"Oh, she is going to check with Aunt Gigi first. She doesn't want to impose on her."

"Will you call me back as soon as you know?"

"Yeah, I promise, Cat. Well, talk to you later. Bye."

"Okay, bye, Derek. But don't forget to call me," Cat added excited over the prospect.

Laura waited for Derek to hang up the phone then said, "Listen, Derek, you shouldn't be inviting your friends over to your aunt's house without her permission. She is old and cannot watch over everyone."

"Oh, no Mom, I didn't invite Cat. He invited himself. I guess I shouldn't have told him about the delicious snacks that Aunt Gigi makes. Now he really wants to go there."

"Hmm, I see. What kind of snacks does she make?"

Derek repeated what he told Cat about the myriad snacks that they had eaten at Aunt Gigi's.

Laura raised her eyebrows in surprise. "Does that mean that my snacks aren't up to par?"

"Umm, oh no, Mom. Your snacks rock!" Derek didn't meet his mother's eyes as he ran up the stairs to the safety of his brother's room.

Derek ran so fast that he nearly tripped and fell at the top of the stairs as

Davey looked out in surprise when he heard the thundering feet.

"Where are you going in such a hurry? Are you in trouble with Mom?"

"No, but I could have been if I hadn't escaped fast enough." Derek relayed what transpired during and after the phone call to Cat.

"Oh, boy, Derek. You know how sensitive Mom is about her food, snacks included," Davey said as he tried not to laugh out loud.

"Is Mom going to call Aunt Gigi about Cat going to her house, Derek?"

"Yeah, I guess she will. Well, I hope she will or Cat is going to be awfully disappointed if he can't go with us tomorrow."

"But how are we going to do our magic with Aunt Gigi or use the crystal ball and talk to Mianna? This is not a good idea, Bro."

"Yeah, I shouldn't have encouraged Cat by telling him about the snacks, huh?"

"Well, duh!" Davey expressed his exasperation.

"Maybe I should just call Cat back and tell him that Aunt Gigi said 'no'."

"You could, but what if you call her and ask her yourself, Derek? Maybe she can come up with a solution where we can do magic and have Cat there too."

"How would we do that? Cat would see everything and then really bug us about magic."

"Ha, could be a bigger problem. But it's worth a try, right? All she could say is 'no' which is what we are expecting anyway."

"I better see if Mom called her already before I do that," Derek retorted.

Derek walked back downstairs hesitantly looking around toward the kitchen where his mother was working.

"Hey, Mom, did you call Aunt Gigi yet?"

"No, I didn't. Why? Are you in a hurry or do you want me to burn dinner?"

"Umm, no to both questions, Mom. But…umm can I call her and ask her myself?"

"Are you sure you want to do that? Are you prepared to have her tell you 'no'?"

"Yes, Mom. But I think she may surprise us both and say 'yes'."

"Okay, go head, but be nice and polite when you ask."

"Sure Mom, I'm always polite with Aunt Gigi," Derek reported leaving out what happened when they pushed Aunt Gigi too much recently. It was something that they wanted to forget.

CHAPTER SIX

Back on the Case

Derek was relieved after he spoke with Aunt Gigi. She seemed so sweet and accepting of having Cat over.

Derek had asked her politely and that is what must have made her say 'yes'.

"Well, what did she say?" Davey was at the bottom of the stairs waiting to find out the results of Derek's call.

"I can't believe it, but Aunt Gigi said 'yes' and seemed happy to have Cat come over."

"Can you believe that? I really thought she would give me a harder time before agreeing so easily. She must have something up her sleeve," Derek surmised.

"Oh boy, I wonder what?" Davey queried clearly worried.

"Do you want to call Cat or should I, Derek?"

"I'll call him. He's expecting me to call back, Davey. Besides I want to hear the surprise in his voice."

"Hi Cat. Good news, you can come over to Aunt Gigi's with us tomorrow."

"Really, you're kidding, right? Don't tease me, Derek. My mouth is salivating waiting for some of your aunt's delicious snacks."

"Ha! No kidding, Cat. She really said okay," Derek sniggered clearly enjoying Cat's response.

***

The next morning the twins headed out and met Cat at their aunt's house. He was anxiously waiting out front for them to come.

"Hey Cat, were you waiting long?" the twins chirped together.

"Yeah, I got here twenty minutes ago. Couldn't wait any longer at home.

Mom told me to go on ahead. I was driving her crazy pacing around."

"Sounds like you, Cat. You never sit still," Davey snorted.

"Come this way, Cat, and put your bike under the stairs here. We always keep them out of sight in case someone tries to steal them. It's safer that way."

"Good idea, guys! There's room for three or more," Cat announced as he looked around the back yard.

"So where did you first see the dog?"

"See the garden over there. The dog ran along the edge of the garden and went into the high grass and trees," Derek pointed at the woods.

"Maybe we should go look in the woods. He might still be hiding out," Cat declared.

"Nah, let's go see Aunt Gigi. She's waiting for us and probably watching our every move right now," Derek reported.

"What, what did you say, Derek?"

Davey used "TT" to stop Derek from saying too much about their aunt.

Derek responded, *oh yeah, I almost forgot, Davey. Thanks for stopping me. I may have said something about her powers.*

Cat looked between the boys, shrugged his shoulders and followed them up the stairs.

Davey rang the bell and waited as he looked around once more for some sign of the brown scraggly dog.

Aunt Gigi appeared at the door and exclaimed, "Hi boys, so nice to see you. You brought your friend with you today. How lovely. What is your name young man?"

"Umm, Mickey, Mickey Catonni. Hi."

"Hello, Mickey. It's nice to meet you. Well come on in boys. I have some snacks ready in the kitchen."

Mickey's eyes got bigger as he followed closely behind the boys and Aunt Gigi.

Davey and Derek shared "TT" as they walked toward the laden table covered with more snacks then they had ever seen before.

It looks like Aunt Gigi is trying to impress Cat.

Observing Cat, Derek agreed.

I think Aunt Gigi has definitely succeeded.

The boys sat and filled up sampling everything as Aunt Gigi smiled with satisfaction.

"Well, have you had enough to eat, boys?"

"Yep, it was delicious. Everything that Derek told me is true about your snacks," Cat announced.

"Is that so?" Aunt Gigi chuckled as she looked at the twins and winked.

"Well, why don't we sit in the living room and talk about the dog."

Davey's head swiveled in Derek's directions and used "TT" to alert him about something happening.

What is Aunt Gigi going to say in front of Cat? Is she going to share Mianna's findings? How will she do that?

I don't know, Davey. She'll have to erase Cat's memory like she did with the boys in our last case. Oh boy, things are going to get crazy.

Aunt Gigi watched the twins share their thoughts and waited for them to stop before saying, "Well, boys, have a seat on the couch and I will explain what I found out about the dog."

Cat looked around the room and let out a gasp as he spotted the numerous figurines and other paraphernalia from Aunt Gigi's and Uncle George's travels.

Davey and Derek smiled in appreciation as they were proud of the items that their aunt and uncle had collected over their many years of travel. They watched Cat as he moved closer to the shelves to get a better view of everything.

Aunt Gigi cleared her throat and announced, "Boys, I'm waiting. Please sit down."

Cat jumped up in alarm and ran over to the couch and sat next to the twins who were looking a little anxious too.

"There, now I can begin," Aunt Gigi chortled.

"My friend, Mianna, has been busy keeping her eyes on the dog. She reported that he lives a few miles from here in a little house in the woods. There seemed to be no one around and the house didn't look lived in, at least lately, that is." Aunt Gigi winked at the twins before going on.

Davey and Derek shared "TT" back and forth as they waited for more information from their aunt. They each held their breath as they observed Aunt Gigi's winking and knowing smile that she was aware of their anxiety.

Mickey looked at the twins and Aunt Gigi and waited for a chance to interrupt. "Umm, excuse me, but who is Mianna?"

The boys gulped and waited for Aunt Gigi to answer.

"Oh, Mianna, is a dear old friend of mine. So sorry that I didn't explain that to you first before beginning, Mickey."

"Oh okay. Sorry to interrupt." Mickey sat back and waited for more information.

CHAPTER SEVEN

More Information Coming

Davey couldn't hold his tongue any longer and ventured, "Aunt Gigi, did Mianna say anything else about the dog? Where is his owner?"

"Ah, my impatient nephew, she did tell me that the dog had free rein in and out of the house through his doggy door. There has been no sign of anyone around the house. But I plan to make a visit soon to find out about the owner. Don't you worry I will get to the bottom of this concern of yours."

"Thank you, Aunt Gigi. But I just want to make sure that the dog is not alone and in danger of any kind. He could starve to death if he doesn't have anyone to take care of him."

Derek nodded in agreement as Aunt Gigi gave the twins one of her sweet smiles that held a lot of promise for success in her goal.

"No worries, my dears. I will keep you up-to-date on what I find out. Okay?"

Turning toward Mickey, Aunt Gigi gave him one of her disarming grins and asked, "Well, Mickey, what would you like to know about me or my lovely collection? I noticed that you have been examining them from afar. Would you like to come a little closer to get a better look?"

"Oh yes, Ma'am. I would love to see them close up. They're awesome! I especially love the swords on the wall over there. Where did you get them?"

Mickey's eyes lit up as he moved forward for a closer look. His hands edged upwards but did not touch the swords.

"Oh, they are a little souvenir when we went to Spain. They are swords that the bull fighters use to kill the bulls. Would you like to touch them, Mickey?"

An audible gasp was heard from Mickey as he looked in awe at the swords and waited patiently for a chance to touch them.

"Oh, please, Ma'am, I would love to touch them. They kill bulls with these?" Mickey's voice shook in anticipation.

"Yes, they do. Why of course, dear boy. Please put out your hands and I will place them carefully there. You must not move your hands or touch the blades. They are extremely sharp. Do you understand, Mickey?"

"Oh, yes, Ma'am. I understand."

The twins stood alongside Cat as they observed his face, white as a ghost. He looked like he was in shock. Cat's eyes were glazed over as he held out his hands and Aunt Gigi placed her swords there.

"TT" was shared. *Davey, look at Cat's face. Did Aunt Gigi put him in a trance? He never stands still or quiet this long. Something is wrong.*

Yeah, I know. Look at his eyes! They are opened wide and he is staring at the swords but not blinking.

The twins were so busy talking to each other in their heads that they did not see Aunt Gigi creep up behind them. They nearly jumped out of their skins.

"What, what's wrong?" Derek yelped out.

"Oh sorry to make you jump, Derek. You both were in another world and I wanted to get your attention. I see that you noticed your friend. Don't worry, Mickey is busy for the time being. He will not hear us or see anything. So, why don't we get back to your lessons? I have more to teach you today."

"But what about…," Davey interrupted.

"Oh, Mickey is fine. Don't worry about him. I will take him out of the trance once we are finished. Are you both ready?"

Davey jumped in and responded, "Oh yes, Aunt Gigi. Let's get on with the lesson. What do you have to teach us today?"

"Well, you seemed interested in time travel last time you were here. This will be more like moving in the present though. If you remember, I did mention that I wanted to take a closer look at the house where the dog lives. How would you like to learn the spell to take us there?"

Derek looked with surprise at his aunt and couldn't get his voice to respond.

Davey pounced on the chance to answer for them both. "Wow, really, Aunt Gigi? We are actually going to learn how to time travel together? So cool! Mom will love this!"

Aunt Gigi didn't respond back as quickly as the twins thought she would but instead just stared at them.

"What…what's wrong, Aunt Gigi?" Davey ventured to ask since Derek was still in shock.

"I think we better not share this with your mother just yet. Let's get it perfected first. We may have some mishaps and I don't want Laura to worry too much over you two. I promised her to take good care of you which I am and will continue to do."

"Oh, okay, Aunt Gigi. We won't say anything if we have any mishaps 'cause we know how Mom worries about everything!" Davey chortled.

"That's my boy! You will have plenty to share with her once we get all the bugs ironed out of this spell, I assure you."

Derek at this point was still standing perfectly still with his mouth wide open and eyes staring straight ahead almost like Cat.

Davey poked his brother in the side and pushed his arm to get him to respond.

When nothing worked to wake up his brother from this stupor, Aunt Gigi stepped in and whispered in his ear, "Wake up Derek."

"Huh, what did you say, Aunt Gigi?" Derek finally responded.

"Ah, there you are. Did I frighten you with the idea of this new spell, dear?"

"Oh, no, I don't know what happened to me. I couldn't answer you. That is really strange, isn't it? I am never at a loss for words, right Davey?"

"Yeah, that's for sure!" Davey tittered.

"Now boys, let's begin, shall we? Are you ready?"

"Yes, yes, we are ready! Come on, Derek. Are you with us or not?" Davey stressed as he poked his brother once again.

"Hey, quit poking me, Davey! I'm as ready as I'll ever be!"

Aunt Gigi left the living room to inform George about Mickey and not to worry that they would be back shortly. She also retrieved the twins' wands on her way back to the living room and handed them to the boys as she began her tutorial.

"You must listen carefully to my every word with this spell. One wrong word and we could end up in...well, let's just say we could go somewhere where we don't want to go."

"Hmm, interesting, Aunt Gigi. Did you and your sister ever use this spell to go somewhere and ended up somewhere else by mistake?" Derek asked, his curiosity getting the better of him.

"Well, I guess you could say that."

The twins waited for some further information from their aunt but to no avail.

"Let's just say that's another story to tell you some other time," Aunt Gigi cackled.

Hearing this strange cackle from her made the boys exchange worried looks and stand up tall and pay attention as she started their place travel lessons.

"Take your wands in your right hand and follow my movements exactly. I will say the words and you repeat one word at a time, individually please."

The boys nodded in agreement and they held their wands like instructed. Davey decided to go first, being the oldest, and waited for the first words from Aunt Gigi.

"ehT esuoh no 01 eniregnaT enaL si erehw I tnaw ot og."

Davey carefully repeated each word slowly to get it right then waited for further instructions.

"Good, Davey, good job! Now Derek, repeat this same sentence after me."

Derek repeated each word putting emphasis on the ending.

"Wonderful, Derek, another commendable job!"

Both boys beamed with pleasure and pride at their Aunt.

"Here is the second half of the spell. You must listen first to me and after you will repeat each word together. I want us to go all together and not one at a time. Do you understand?"

"Yes," the boys answered.

"tfiL em pu tub esaelp og wols."

The boys repeated each word after their aunt as she reached forward on the last word to grab hold of their hands. Before they knew what was happening they were whisked away through a swirling tunnel of colors and vibrations.

The boys held tightly to their aunt's hands as they felt as if they were going to be sick. They shut their eyes and said silent prayers through "TT" that they would always be good from now on if they could survive this spell.

Just as they thought they would pass out their feet hit grass and they bounced up and down on the balls of their feet as their aunt held them upright.

"There, you did it, boys! How about that for magic?" Aunt Gigi's face crinkled up in a broad smile.

The twins were still shaking but standing on their own now. Through more "TT" the boys exclaimed their joy and surprise at their accomplishment.

Wow, can you believe it, Davey? We did it! We did it! That was so cool I want to do it again.

Yeah, it was way cool, Bro! I didn't know where we were for a little while. The colors were spinning around and the vibrations were banging against my head. It felt like I had a set of drums going off in my head! Did you feel that, Derek?

Yeah, I felt it too. But then it passed and all I felt was a strong wind pushing us ahead through a tunnel of colors. No one would believe this! I don't believe this! Wow!

I wonder if we would have gotten lost in the tunnel without Aunt Gigi to hold onto and direct us. She kept us standing upright. I think we would have fallen over from being so dizzy.

Yeah, Davey, I guess that's why we have to do it together for a while until we get out all the bugs like Aunt Gigi said.

Aunt Gigi's voice could be heard as the boys suddenly stopped talking in their heads. "Well, boys, what do you think about this spell? Are you feeling okay? Still dizzy and disoriented?"

"Umm, not anymore, Aunt Gigi. At first I felt as if I was going to upchuck. You know what I mean?"

"Yes, Davey, I do know what that feels like. When I was your age I felt the same way. But now I am used to it and keep my head up and look straight ahead and now I don't get dizzy or sick to my stomach. With practice you both will learn how to do this. Maybe next time we will have travel first, snacks second."

"The snacks were great for either time, Aunt Gigi. But, I sure hope things get easier on my stomach," Derek exclaimed, "but it was so cool, Aunt Gigi. I can't wait to do it again."

"We will be doing it again shortly after we finish our task here."

CHAPTER EIGHT

Tangerine Lane

After getting their feet planted on the lawn from their place travel the boys moved along behind Aunt Gigi toward the house. Aunt Gigi looked around up and down the street before venturing closer to the house to make sure no one was in the vicinity to observe them.

"What's wrong, Aunt Gigi?" Davey asked.

"Oh, nothing, Davey. I want to make sure we are alone and no one is watching us."

"Is there some danger here?" Derek responded as he whipped his head back and forth.

Please stay close to me as we get near the house."

Davey and Derek used "TT" to share their concerns as they followed their aunt.

Do you think Aunt Gigi saw something? She was nervous and she never gets nervous. Did you notice that, Derek?

Yeah, I did. She's making me nervous too! What if we have to get out of here fast? Will she be able to take us back to her house quickly? I know we take too long to do a spell. We can't do it alone.

Of course not, Bro. We're novices and she's the pro. Don't worry so much. We'll be fine. Just watch where you're going, okay, Derek? You just missed that tree!

Yeah, I saw it! Stop pushing me along. Shh! Did you hear something?

"Boys, stop right here. Let me knock on the door and see if anyone answers. You stay at the bottom of the stairs in case you need to run and hide."

"What, run and hide? What do you mean run and hide? Where are we going to go?" Derek was shaking from head to toe.

"What's going to happen, Aunt Gigi?" Davey voiced his concern too.

"Nothing, dear boys. I just want you to be alert and stop talking inside your heads. It distracts you."

"Okay, Aunt Gigi. Sorry," both boys agreed and didn't dare look at each other for fear of doing "TT" again.

Aunt Gigi stood at the door and knocked twice and listened. She tried again but no sounds were coming from within. She tried the doorknob and turned it. The door opened with a jarring sound and Aunt Gigi peeked in and stepped into the room.

The boys looked on in anticipation from the bottom of the stairs but didn't move as commanded. They held their breaths as they saw their aunt disappear into the dark interior of the house.

What was only a few minutes seemed like much more to the boys as they waited for their aunt to appear again. Aunt Gigi's head poked out and she smiled to ease the boys' nerves.

"It's okay, no worries, boys. No one is home. Let's get back before anyone notices us here."

Grabbing the boys' hands Aunt Gigi recanted her spell and they were once again traveling through time and space in a tunnel of wind and colors.

This time the travel appeared to be smoother and faster than before much to the surprise and relief of the boys. They didn't have the pounding in their heads or the upset stomachs for which they were grateful.

Arriving in their Aunt Gigi's living room where they had begun was a welcome respite for the boys. They were still feeling shaky and not sure of what to expect next.

Aunt Gigi told the boys, "Relax and sit down. There's nothing to be concerned about. No one was home. I didn't go through the whole house but I did call out and no one answered. I used my powers to look around without moving forward. Someone is definitely living there. I will have to ask Mianna to keep a lookout for the dog and for anyone coming and going into the house."

"Aunt Gigi, what about Mickey? He's still in a trance holding the swords," Davey mentioned in warning.

"Oh, yes, of course, Davey. I haven't forgotten him. Let's talk a little before I take him out of his trance, shall we?"

"Umm, sure, Aunt Gigi," Derek looked at Davey and shrugged his shoulders.

"Let's review what we know so far, boys. First we know where the dog lives and that he has an owner, or did have one. Second we need to find the owner and find out if he is injured. As I am sure you noticed, the dog had blood on his paw which was not his. It could belong to his owner or maybe someone else."

"Yes, but how do we find the owner of the dog? Where do we begin?" Derek probed.

"Well, I will contact Mianna again and see if she has found out anything to help us. Then I will decide where to proceed," Aunt Gigi countered.

"Can we do anything to help, Aunt Gigi?" Davey inquired.

"You can keep your eyes and ears open and if you hear anything about others seeing this dog let me know."

"Okay, Aunt Gigi. We will ask around and keeps our eyes and ears open," Derek smiled at his brother as he answered.

Davey nodded and "TT" was exchanged, *EEO (eyes, ears, open) Derek! Did you hear that? We can at least tell Cat that part of the conversation.*

Yeah, but not much else. Oops, Aunt Gigi is waiting for us to listen up again.

"All right boys. Let's get your friend back to the present and then you can all be on your way home. Let your friend know only that we are still looking for clues as to where the dog is. Okay?"

"Okay, sure, Aunt Gigi," both boys nodded in agreement.

In the next few seconds Mickey was back to normal and blinking and yawning and stretching his stiff limbs. He had a surprised look on his face that he had to do all this.

"Hey, Cat...I mean, Mickey, what's wrong?" the twins asked their bewildered friend and fellow junior detective.

"I...I don't know. I feel a little tired and stiff as if I have not moved in a long time. But that can't be. We have only been here for half an hour. Strange, very strange, huh?"

"Yeah that is strange, Mickey. Are you ready to head home?"

"What, we just got here, guys. Why are we going home already? We didn't get to discuss what we need to do to find the dog."

"Well you must have fallen asleep because we already discussed it all. We've been here for a few hours already," Derek said.

"Are you kidding me, Derek? Davey, is he crazy or something?"

"Umm, well, umm, we have been here a while, Mickey. I guess you must have taken a nap. That's why you are so tired and stiff."

The twins looked toward their aunt for help when they were at a loss for words to explain things to Mickey.

"Ahh, Mickey my boy, everything is okay. You did take a little nap. Maybe it was all the snacks you ate that made you sleepy. Don't worry, the boys will fill you in about what we discussed on your way home. Okay guys, time to go. I need to check on Uncle George. He has been working in the garden all afternoon. He tends to do too much," Aunt Gigi tutted as she headed out the back door and waved to the boys.

"Okay, if you say so. I must have slept. Boy, I've never done that before," Mickey followed the twins out the door and jumped on his bike still shaking his head to clear it.

The twins shared "TT", *Davey, I'm worried about Cat. He doesn't seem to be awake yet. Look at him. He is still looking out of it and shaking his head to clear out the fog.*

I know. Should we ask Aunt Gigi to do something? He may get into an accident riding his bike in this state.

As they boys rode up the street Aunt Gigi appeared behind them and waved her hand toward Mickey to help clear his mind. She knew that he was still foggy. She had kept him under the spell too long and was upset with herself. It would not happen again, she mused.

Davey looked over at Mickey as he was suddenly riding faster. He finally was back to normal.

"Hey, Cat, are you okay?"

"Yeah, why wouldn't I be okay, Davey?"

"Well, you did seem a bit confused and sleepy back at Aunt Gigi's."

"Really, I don't feel sleepy now. Are you guys going to fill me in on what you decided to do about the dog and his owner?"

"Oh, yeah, let's stop up there and talk about it," Davey yelled over to Derek to slow down and stop at the bench up ahead.

"So what did I miss, guys?" Cat voiced his concern.

The twins simultaneously filled Cat in on what they could share as per their aunt's request leaving out the travel spell.

"That's not telling me anything I didn't already know. How are we going to find the owner or the dog? The dog has disappeared too."

"Cat, do you remember we said to use EEO (eyes and ears open) in our last case? Now is the time to do that again," Derek responded with a chuckle.

"Okay, I am good at that! I sometimes think I have extra eyes and ears because I hear and see things others don't," Cat laughed as he got back onto his bike.

"Let's race to the next block before we turn to go to our separate ways, okay?" Cat challenged.

"Let's go!" the twins yelled together as they raced ahead of Cat, giggling all the way.

CHAPTER NINE

A Step Back

"See you tomorrow, Cat. If you find out anything about the case let us know ASAP, okay?"

"Of course, guys. I'm with you on this. You know me, ready, willing and aiming to please!" Cat guffawed as he waved goodbye.

The boys slapped hands and turned home finishing up their race in a tie.

Derek, as usual, was amused by his friend and snickered all the way home.

Davey was thinking things over and ready to make his list on their busy marker board. He was so deep in thought that he didn't see his brother pass him and pull into their opened garage.

"Hey, Bro, I beat you this time! Ha! I finally beat you for once!" Derek was jumping up and down with a wide smile on his face.

"What, oh yeah. I let you win!" Davey smirked back.

"No you didn't I won fair and square!"

Their voices were rising as their mother opened the door from the kitchen and peered out at them.

"Hey you two. What's going on? Get yourselves in here. I need some help."

"TT" was shared, *now you did it, Derek! You made so much noise we'll have to help Mom with something. I hope it's not the laundry again! I hate to fold clothes!*

Me? You were the one who was making so much noise because you thought you beat me!

Well, I did beat you!

Whatever! Ha, piece of cake, Derek. You will have more to fold too! You make a mess out of your clothes. Everything is always inside out!

The twins reluctantly trudged into the kitchen to see what they had to do.

"Well, there you are. I thought you would never get in here," Laura said clearly exasperated.

"Sorry, Mom," Davey apologized.

"Yeah, sorry, Mom," Derek responded in kind.

"Listen boys, please sit down. Aunt Gigi just called me. She told me that you had a new lesson today about place travel."

The boys' eyes widened in surprise and a loud intake of breath was heard from both of them.

Using "TT" they shared their shock over their mother's words. *I can't believe it! Aunt Gigi told us not to share this with Mom and then she shared it with her! Why did she do that?*

I don't know, Davey. It's confusing. Maybe she wanted to be the one to break the news to Mom. Aunt Gigi was afraid that we would embellish the spell too much and scare Mom, I guess.

Yeah, maybe that's it! But what do we tell her? Does she know everything about the dangers?

Your guess is as good as mine. Let her tell us what she knows. Why don't you ask her, Derek?

"Mom, what did Aunt Gigi tell you about our place travel?"

"She told me everything. Now I need to tell you one thing. This is extremely important, boys. Are you listening?"

"Yes," both boys answered.

"I know how dangerous this spell can be. You must pay close attention to Aunt Gigi. My mother told me one time that she tried this spell with her sisters, Gigi and Auriana, and almost got lost in a strange place. If not for the help of her sisters to pull her back she would have been lost forever. Do you understand? The only thing about this travel is that you are only moving in present time. Aunt Gigi did assure me that it's not dangerous like the time travel is."

"Oh, wow, we didn't know that, Mom. How old was Grandma when that happened?" Davey ventured.

"She was about your age. That is why I am stressing this. I don't want anything to happen to you. You are too precious to me." Laura wiped away a tear.

"Oh, Mom! Don't get upset. We're going to listen to Aunt Gigi. Don't worry," Davey reassured.

The boys hugged their mother and reiterated that they were going to be careful with any new spells they learned.

Laura sighed, wiped away another tear and hugged the boys back. Releasing them she told them, "All right boys, get cleaned up and set the table for me." She proceeded to start dinner after feeling a sense of relief.

The twins rushed through cleaning up and setting the table so they could go to their rooms and get down to business on their new case. They felt as if they had taken a step back and had lost some time.

Standing in front of the marker board in Davey's room Derek listed what they knew so far according to Aunt Gigi which wasn't very much.

Davey stood back and reviewed the list. "Hmm, looks like we need to do some digging around the dog's neighborhood. Maybe one of the neighbors knows something."

"I agree, but we don't know where the house is. Remember how we got there before? We can't do that again by ourselves. Mom would have a fit and Aunt Gigi would…well, we don't know what Aunt Gigi would do to us if we tried that spell on our own."

"Davey, I don't think I would be able to do it without Aunt Gigi. We could get lost like Grandma almost did and besides, we can't do it without our wands."

"Yeah, you're right. But what are you frightened about, Derek?" Davey pushed forward.

"Nothing, Davey, I would do it if I had my wand but I don't know if I remember how."

"Do you remember, Davey?"

"Not really but we could Google the address and ride our bikes over to the house and nose around."

"Oh, you mean we won't have to use the spell. Well, now you're talking. I can do that!" Derek was excited to begin their adventure.

"Okay, Bro, let the adventure begin! Google away and let's make plans for tomorrow. We can call Cat and the three of us can canvas the neighborhood. We can make up a story that we are looking for odd jobs for the summer to earn some spending money."

"That could work, maybe," Davey replied.

The boys sat in front of their parent's computer screen and memorized the directions to 10 Tangerine Lane. It was near the park, lucky for them.

"Let's go after dinner. It's light until almost eight. We could say we are going to the park with Cat. It's not lying really, right, Bro?"

"Derek, all we have to do is tell Mom we are going to the park. Then we can nose around the neighborhood. That way we're not lying. Don't forget to call Cat."

"Okay, I'll call Cat but don't look Mom in the eye when you ask her about going to the park."

"Huh, me! Yeah, right!" Davey rolled his eyes.

CHAPTER TEN

Using EEO

The three boys raced all the way to the park and slowed down when they got closer to Tangerine Lane. They looked up and down to make sure no one was watching them.

"Hey Cat, why don't you take the houses across the street from Sandy's house? Davey, you take the houses on the right side of Sandy's house and I..."

"Sandy? Who in the world is Sandy?" Davey yelled stopping his brother in mid-stream.

"Oh, I thought it was a good name for the dog. I think once he's cleaned up he'll probably be sandy colored."

"Do you really?" Davey asked, his voice rising.

Cat chuckled once he saw Davey's face. He sat back on his bike and waited for a confrontation.

"Well, don't you think it's a good name for him?" Derek probed as he watched his brother's face for acceptance.

"You have no right to name a dog that is not yours. He already has a name, don't you think?"

"Yeah, probably does. But I thought…"

"No don't do this, Derek. You know what will happen when you set your mind on getting something. You will be disappointed. We don't know anything about the owner."

"I know, Davey, but I really like this dog and am worried that he's alone. What if something happened to the owner? Then, the dog will need a home."

"But, Derek, you know Mom. She won't let us have a dog because she thinks we won't take care of it."

"But I will take care of it. I promise."

"Don't tell me this, Derek. I'm not the one you have to convince."

"Hey guys! Are you going to talk all day long or are we going to investigate?" Cat smiled his usual Cheshire cat grin while he waited for a response.

"Okay, let's go. We can talk more about this later, Bro," Davey stressed.

"Okay, I guess," Derek answered reluctantly.

The boys headed off to their allotted houses to start their investigations.

As Davey arrived at the first house next door to the dog's house he parked his bike at the foot of the stairs and walked up to the door. He pressed the doorbell and straightened his t-shirt and tucked it into his jeans.

The door opened and an elderly woman peeked out at him saying, "What do you want young man?"

"Oh, hello Ma'am. My name is Davey and I am looking for a summer job. Do you need anything done around your yard?" Davey waited for an answer before continuing.

"No young man. I do not need any help. My son does all the work around here."

The woman was about to close the door as Davey asked loudly in case the woman couldn't hear him, "Okay, umm, Ma'am, do you know the people who live next door to you? They have a brown scraggly dog. Do you know where the dog is now?"

"What, what did you say about a dog?"

"The dog who lives next door to you, do you know who the owner is?" Davey asked again.

"I haven't seen Mr. Costa in quite some time or his dog. Why are you asking, young man?"

"Well, I saw his dog recently and he appeared to be uncared for and dirty."

"Oh, Mr. Costa always takes care of Aggy."

"Aggy? You mean the dog is a girl? I thought it was a boy," Davey answered clearly disappointed.

"Do you know where Mr. Costa is now?"

"No, like I just said, young man, I don't know where he is. I haven't seen him in a while," the old woman said impatiently as she closed the door on Davey.

Davey was clearly disappointed but at least he learned the owner's name and name and sex of the dog. That would be a surprise to Derek too. He chuckled to himself.

Derek was not having much more luck at this time nor was Cat. They both hit dead ends as to the whereabouts of the owner and his dog. The boys gathered together and compared notes about what the neighbors had told them.

Derek began the conversation, "So what did you find out Bro?"

Davey couldn't wait to tell Derek what the old woman had told him. "I found out the name of the dog, Derek, and his owner. Do you want to know what it is?"

"Yeah, you're going to tell me anyway. What is it?" Derek tried to appear uninterested but he couldn't help himself and waited with baited breath.

"Aggy! You know what that means, Derek! Aggy is a girl!" Davey tried to keep his smirk at bay.

"What, a girl! No, it can't be!" Derek thought it over and quickly recovered. "Well, Sandy would work. It's a boy's or girl's name." Derek snickered back.

"Whatever!" Davey retorted.

"What about you Cat? How did you do?" Derek inquired.

"Well, I didn't find out anything else but I did manage to get a summer job weeding at the yellow house over there. Mrs. Grillo said I start tomorrow," Cat couldn't help wearing a big smile.

"You got to be kidding!" Derek chortled, "Leave it to you to make something out of this wild goose chase!"

"Now I just have to convince my Mom that I can do this. That's another thing that could be a wild goose chase," Cat laughed amused at his own humor.

"Let's get on home. We need more info on this case but it's getting late and we are not going to find out anything more today." Davey jumped on his bike and looked back at the boys to signal them to follow.

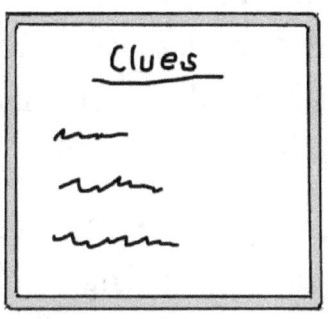

CHAPTER ELEVEN

More Info Needed

Davey faced the marker board and made more notes then turned to Derek for his take on things. "Hey, Derek, what do you think about this case so far? Is there anything else you want to add to the board?"

"Nah, looks like you covered it all including the name of the dog, I see," Derek added reluctantly. He was still unhappy about the fact that the dog was a female.

"We need to go back to the house and look around. Aunt Gigi only looked inside the house. We checked out the neighborhood. What about in the back yard and the woods bordering the house?"

"Yeah, maybe we can go back tomorrow when Cat goes to start his new job weeding. That's too funny to think of Cat doing any kind of work?" Derek giggled and waited for his brother to join in.

"Huh, what did you say?" Davey was lost in thought and wasn't paying attention.

"What's wrong, Davey? It's not like you to daydream. That's my job! I have that perfected if I have to say so myself," Derek guffawed.

"Umm, yep, I was just thinking about going back tomorrow to the house. I have a feeling that we missed something today. The neighbors don't seem to be that worried about Mr. Costa. Don't ya think that's weird?"

"Well, Davey, the neighbors I spoke to seemed to be surprised that they hadn't seen him or the dog. I guess they stay out of other people's business, that's all."

"I can't help feeling that the dog was trying to tell us something. He seemed neglected and dirty. If his owner cared for him so much why was he unkempt?" Davey stressed.

"You got something there, Bro. I agree with you. Let's plan to go back. We can tell Mom we are going back to the park to play ball or something. As long as we don't take too long we can do that."

"How long will it take for us to look around in Mr. Costa's back yard? You can take one part of the yard and woods and look around for something unusual like blood or something," Davey stated.

"Blood? What makes you think we'll find blood?" Derek didn't like this at all.

"The dog did have some blood on his paw. Aunt Gigi said it wasn't his, so it had to be someone else's, don't you think?" Davey continued to explain.

"Do you think…it could be Mr. Costa's? Maybe he's hurt somewhere," Derek hazarded a guess.

"Could be or someone else's," Davey answered not really wanting to know.

"Let's talk more after dinner. Mom just called us to go down," Derek interrupted because his stomach was talking to him.

"All right, but what if we ask Aunt Gigi for some help? She can go with us. We may need to make a getaway fast in case we find something…umm…," Davey hesitated.

"I don't think we should bother Aunt Gigi. Wait a minute! What do you think we are going to find, Davey?"

"Maybe a dead body or something. I don't know. Where did the dog get the blood? It wasn't his," Davey added.

"Oh boy, Bro. We may be in over our heads on this case. We don't deal in murder. We are only kids, for goodness sake!" Derek stressed.

"Are you boys coming today or should I just make you some breakfast?" Laura yelled up the stairs.

"Coming Mom!" the twins answered together.

***

When the twins were quiet through the whole meal, Laura began to worry. Her husband, Donald, didn't seem to be concerned at all. He enjoyed the peace and quiet when he was eating.

Laura waited for Donald to finish and leave the table before she ventured to ask the boys about what was bothering them. She was nervous to ask but needed to know.

"So boys, how is your newest case going?" Laura asked nonchalantly as she could.

"Okay Mom, just the usual stuff," Davey answered.

Derek used "TT" to ask his brother, *are you going to tell Mom anything we found out yet?*

No, not yet. We don't know enough, Derek. After we nose around Mr. Costa's yard then we can tell her what if anything we find.

Okay, if you think we will find something. What if we don't? We still won't know anything of importance to share.

Laura observed the boys quietly talking inside their heads once again. She was always in awe over how they could do that. She waited for a chance to ask another question.

"Don't worry, Mom. We are going to solve the mystery but we just don't know enough to share yet. Okay?" Derek responded knowing his mother needed to know something.

"Okay, if you need to talk to me about anything at all, you know I am here for you both."

"Yup, we know, Mom. Thanks," Davey retorted.

"We need to go upstairs and work on the case more. Okay, Mom?" Derek added as he backed away from the kitchen and put his dish and glass into the dishwasher.

"Go ahead, boys. I'll call you when it's time for dessert after I clean up."

"Oh yeah, call us, Mom. I always want dessert!" Derek sighed thinking about what it could be as he, too, put his dish and glass away as his brother had done.

Tomorrow was going to be a busy day for the boys and a dessert may help give them the needed sugar to have the energy they may need.

CHAPTER TWELVE

What Next

The next morning, after convincing their mother that they were going to check on Mickey at his new job and look around the neighborhood for the dog, they headed out.

As the boys went out the door to the garage to get their bikes their mother yelled, "Stay out of trouble and don't bother any of the neighbors there about the dog."

"Okay, Mom," Davey answered.

The boys went directly to the neighbor's yard to see Cat working away pulling weeds. He was so involved in his task that he didn't realize the twins were standing behind him until Derek spoke.

"Hey Cat, what's ya doing?"

"What...Derek, you scared me out of my mind. What did you do that for?"

"Oh sorry, Cat. I thought you heard us coming up the walk. You really must be into this weeding stuff, huh?"

"Yeah, I really love this stuff! I was just thinking over the case, that's why I didn't hear you. Hey, what are you guys doing here again today? Did you find out anything else?"

"Not really, Cat, but we wanted to check around the yard and woods behind Mr. Costa's house in case there's some evidence of foul play there," Davey replied.

"Wait a minute! What foul play? Do you expect to find a dead body or something?" Cat's voice shook.

"Umm...well, I hope not, Cat, but you never know what we'll find back there. Remember the dog's paw, we told you, had blood on it. It had to come from someone else since it wasn't his," Derek countered in a calm voice.

"Yeah, I remember. But do you think it belongs to, Mr. Costa?"

"Maybe, maybe not," Davey added.

"Well, what do you think, Davey?" Cat was getting anxious to know what was going on.

"You have a lot of weeding to do, Cat. We'll stop by later after we nose around, okay? Don't worry if we find anything, we'll call you," Derek chuckled, clearly getting a kick out of Cat's reaction to this search.

Derek added, "Oh Cat, remember EEO while we are looking around. If you see anyone coming near the house whistle as loud as you can to warn us. Okay?"

"Yeah, okay." Cat sighed heavily as he resumed his weeding.

"Wait a minute, guys. I did see a car slowing down and sitting outside Mr. Costa's house for a few minutes. Then it drove away. I couldn't see the person in the car though."

"Really? Was it a man?" Davey asked intrigued.

"I think so, but I can't be sure."

"Thanks, Cat. Keep a look out for us," Derek quipped.

"Let's go, Derek. We have a lot of area to cover and we don't want to be late going home for lunch."

"Yeah, sure, Bro. I'm right behind you."

Cat turned and watched the twins ride over to the Mr. Costa's house and disappear around the back.

Davey instructed Derek, "You go to the right into the woods and I will take the left side of the yard. If you find anything at all, call me."

"Okay, Davey. You do the same. I mean, call me. You know what I mean." Derek walked away deep in thought.

Davey shook his head and looked around on the grass near the edge of the yard bordering the woods. He headed into the trees and looked closely at an area that seemed to be cleared.

Derek, in the meantime, was deeper into the woods and had bent down to look at something.

Both boys let out yelps as they tried to get each other's attention.

"Davey, come here. I think I found something," he yelled.

Davey looked again at the clearing and yelled back, "Yeah, okay, be right there. I may have found something too."

When Davey came up behind his brother Derek got up and stepped aside so Davey could see what he was looking at.

"What's that?"

"I don't know but it could be some blood. There's a piece of cloth in it," Derek pointed out.

"Yeah, I see the cloth. Looks like it could be from a jacket or shirt. It's plaid."

"What did you find back there, Davey?"

"Oh, I saw a spot that was cleared between the trees with new damp soil. Maybe something was buried there."

"Hmm…what do you make of all this, Davey?"

"I don't know yet but we could try digging up the dirt and see what is buried there."

"Or Maybe we should check with Aunt Gigi. We could stop by her house on the way home and fill her in on what we found," Derek countered.

"Okay, that may be a good idea. She could come back with us through place travel again, or is it *placement travel*? We really are not going backward or forward in time."

"Yeah, I like that *placement travel*. That is a new coined phrase and we did, or you did it, Bro. We could call it PT."

Davey laughed, "You and your acronyms, Derek!"

"Race you to Aunt Gigi's, Derek!" Davey jumped on his bike and raced away much to the chagrin of Derek who was left behind once again.

"Oh for goodness sake, Davey! You don't play fair! I wasn't ready!" Derek grumbled.

CHAPTER THIRTEEN

Aunt Gigi's Plan

Aunt Gigi looked out her front window and saw the boys racing toward her house. She chuckled as she observed their competitiveness.

The twins raced up their aunt's stairs after storing their bikes in the usual place. The door opened as if by magic and their stood Aunt Gigi with a huge smile on her cherubic face.

"Hey boys. What a surprise to see you. I didn't expect to see you today. Why are you in such a hurry?"

"We have a lot to share with you, Aunt Gigi. We went back to the dog's house twice and found out some things."

"Really, twice? What did you find out?" Gigi enquired.

"Well," Davey began, "we went once with Mickey and the second time today, just us."

Derek jumped in and continued, "We canvassed the neighbor's houses saying that we were looking for summer jobs and asked them about Mr. Costa and his dog, Sandy."

"Mr. Costa, Sandy? Are these their names? My, you are quite resourceful young men. I am proud of your accomplishments. It looks like you don't need my help here."

"Well, the dog's name is Aggy not Sandy. Derek named it Sandy."

Derek gave his brother a look of displeasure and audibly grumbled.

Davey ignored him and picked up the explanation, "Well, we do need your help, Aunt Gigi. Today we went back and searched the back yard and the woods bordering the yard." Looking toward Derek he used "TT" to discuss what to say next.

Do you want to explain what you found first, Derek?

Yeah, then you can add in info about the cleared spot.

"Well, I found a piece of cloth that was stained with...looks like something dark like blood."

"Really? Hmm."

"Oh, and Aunt Gigi, I found an area that was cleared and damp like something was buried there."

"Wow, you two have been busy. Looks like we will have to go take a look at these suspicious areas. Are you ready now to take a little trip?"

"We're going now? Okay, I guess, what do you think, Derek?"

"Yes, of course, let's go now!"

"That's what I like, decisiveness!"

"Hang onto my hands boys, we're going for a little ride."

"Yay, let's go!" Derek couldn't contain his enthusiasm. He was beginning to enjoy this way to travel.

The trip seemed to be quicker than last time and the boys held on tight to their aunt's hands as they landed on the back lawn of Mr. Costa's house.

"How did you know we were going to land in the backyard, Aunt Gigi?"

"Skill, my boy, and plenty of practice," Aunt Gigi giggled at the expression of surprise on the twins' faces.

"Now boys let's get to work. Show me what you found."

The boys moved quickly forward until they found the area that was damp and cleared.

Aunt Gigi bent down to take a closer look. She placed her hands on the area and closed her eyes and murmured some soft words.

The twins leaned in and listened but couldn't figure out what she had said. They watched and waited for their aunt to say something.

"Well, it seems that something is buried here. Nice work, boys."

"Huh, what? Something is buried here? What? What is buried here?" Derek shouted a little too loudly.

"Shh, Derek, no need to shout."

"Aunt Gigi, what is buried here? Could it be Mr. Costa?" Davey asked in a quieter voice.

"No, dear boys. It is not a person. It appears to be a rabbit. Maybe it was a pet. Let's move on to the other thing you found."

"Oh, yes. I found a piece of stained cloth," Derek exclaimed as he ran ahead to find it.

When he arrived at the spot the cloth was gone. He looked around the area and moved out further to search but couldn't find it.

"Oh no, it's gone! How could it have disappeared unless...someone took it?"

"It's okay, Derek. Let's keep looking. Maybe you made a mistake and it's not here. Maybe it's further over there," Davey pointed in another direction and answered in a soft voice in an attempt to calm his brother down.

"Derek, please take my hand and stand still and a take a deep breath. Think carefully, where were you standing when you found the cloth? Close your eyes and look inside you and you will find it," Aunt Gigi explained.

Derek placed his hand in Aunt Gigi's and took a deep breath and closed his eyes. He could see himself walking around and stooping down to examine the ground and then gasping as he made his discovery.

"Yes, I see it now. It's over there in between the trees." Derek ran over to the area and dropped down to look closely. There was the piece of stained cloth right where he had found it.

"Yay, I found it! It's here. Come quickly and look, Aunt Gigi!"

"Ah, yes I see it my boy. You are a good detective. Well, you both are for that matter. I am proud of both of you."

"I knew you could find it, Derek," Davey exclaimed proudly patting his brother on the back.

"Yeah, I did too, Bro. Well, you did a good job finding that grave even if it wasn't Mr. Costa in it. Ugh, what a thought!" Davey shook his head in disgust.

While the boys were congratulating one another Aunt Gigi was reciting an incantation over the cloth after which she picked it up with her gloved hands and tucked it into her pocket.

CHAPTER FOURTEEN

Examining the clues

Davey looked over at Aunt Gigi and let out a gasp and quickly shared "TT" with his brother.

Derek, look at Aunt Gigi! She is doing something magical without her wand. The cloth is moving!

Yeah, I see it, Davey! I wouldn't have believed you if I hadn't seen it too with my own eyes! What do you think she is doing?

I don't know, Little Bro, but maybe she is trying to find the rest of the shirt that goes with the piece. Maybe she can even talk to cloth!?

Ha, that is too funny, Davey! You can't be serious, are you?

Well, you know the powers Aunt Gigi has. I believe she can do the impossible.

Yeah, you may be right, Bro.

Aunt Gigi stood up and turned toward the boys who she knew were getting impatient and curious.

"Well, boys, it seems that this cloth has only been here for a couple of days. If someone is injured they may be nearby in need of help. Let's move out a little further into the woods. If you would both rather stay here I can do it myself."

"Oh no, we want to go too, right, Davey?"

"Yes, yes we want to go too, Aunt Gigi. Maybe we'll find Mr. Costa. He may be hurt somewhere out in the woods and needs our help."

"That's my boys! Well, let's go."

The threesome trudged through the high grass and then through the tightly packed trees until they came to a hill. They looked down the knoll before starting to descend slowly. It was quite steep and they were not too sure of foot with all the rocks and pebbles that were lining the slope.

As they continued to descend they spotted something moving in the brush ahead. Out it came heading right for them. It was the brown scraggly dog. He was agitated and barked as he jumped up and down in front of them.

Aunt Gigi raised her hand over the dog and he suddenly quieted down and sat at her feet looking at her in attention.

She whispered to the dog and he turned and ran ahead. The twins followed behind their aunt as they quickened their pace.

The dog began to bark more excitedly now as they came closer to her. The dog was looking down at something in between the large rocks and grass.

As they moved in for a better look they saw a man lying on his side as if he was sleeping. The dog laid down next to the man and snuggled close to him.

Aunt Gigi bent down to examine the man and feel his pulse. She announced, "He's alive but barely. The dog has kept him warm otherwise he might have died from being out in the elements. He looks like he could have slipped down the hill and hit his head.

The twins looked at the man and noticed his head was matted with dried blood. Aunt Gigi must be right.

Aunt Gigi pulled something out of her wrap and put it to her ear. The boys looked on in amazement as they shared "TT".

Oh my God, Davey, Aunt Gigi has a cell phone. Who would have thought?!

Yeah, but she can't call Mianna to make a call to the police, can she? Ha!

All right wise guy!

Davey couldn't help but laugh at his brother's naiveté.

"Hello, this is Grisela Cornbloom. Please send an ambulance to 10 Tangerine Way. There is a man at the bottom of a ravine who is injured."

Hearing only their aunt's side of the conversation. The boys surmised that the police were asking her about how she found the man and his injuries.

"No, sorry I do not know. I was just passing by and a dog led me to the man."

"Yes, of course." Aunt Gigi hung up the phone and looked at the boys.

"An ambulance is on its way."

147

"Aunt Gigi, do we have to stay here until the ambulance comes?"

"Yes, Davey, we do, otherwise they will not know where Mr. Costa is."

"Can we go see Mickey who's working across the street pulling weeds?"

"Well, okay but don't go too far and come right back. I need to take you both home or your mother will be worried."

Davey and Derek ran across the street as fast as they could to report to Cat what had just transpired. They knew he would be upset if he was left out of the loop of the latest developments of the case.

A siren was heard in the distance which alerted Cat before the boys could reach him.

"Hey, what's going on? What are you guys doing here? And where did you come from?"

Not wanting to answer Cat's last question Derek proceeded to explain, "Hi Cat, that's why we came over to talk to you. Aunt Gigi came with us to check out the clues we found the other day, remember we told you about them?"

"Oh, yeah, the grave and the bloody cloth, yes, I remember. What's going on now? Does this siren have something to do with what's going on?" Cat's eyes were wide in anticipation of the news.

"Yes, Aunt Gigi called the police."

"And, what did she find? Why do you guys do this to me, leave me in suspense?" Cat was getting antsy.

"Davey, can I tell him?"

"All right, go ahead but I will interrupt if you don't get it right."

"Cat, we found Mr. Costa and Sandy, err, I mean Aggy. He fell down a ravine in the back of his yard and hit his head."

"Is he…umm…you know," Cat stuttered too frightened to finish his thoughts.

"No, he's alive but just barely," Davey added not waiting for Derek to finish the story.

"Hey, Davey, you didn't let me finish."

"Go ahead finish. But there isn't anything else to tell right now."

"Aww, but we still don't know how he fell and why he was out there to begin with," Derek stressed.

The ambulance pulled up and the boys ran over to them and directed the EMTs to the back of the house. They pulled out a stretcher and hurried through the yard to where Aunt Gigi met them along with Aggy.

The EMTs carried Mr. Costa away to the ambulance and with siren going they headed to the hospital. The police pulled up as they left and Aunt Gigi came over to talk with them.

"Hello, officers. I am the person who called to report this injury. What else do you need from me?"

Aunt Gigi explained once again how she found the man. She gave the police her phone number and address so they could contact her if they needed to speak with her further.

Once the police drove away Aunt Gigi took the boys by the hands and led them back to the yard in amongst the trees. She performed PT and got the boys back to her house without anyone seeing them. She instructed the boys to ride their bikes home and she would follow in her car.

Aunt Gigi went inside their house with the twins and spoke with Laura about what had happened as the boys stood by and listened.

"Hi Laura, sorry to drop in unannounced but I wanted to make sure the boys got back safely. We had a little excitement." Aunt explained what they had found and how the man was in the hospital at present.

"Oh my goodness, are you all okay?"

"Oh yes, we are all fine. Poor Mr. Costa is in bad shape though. Hopefully he will recover."

"Thank God for that. What happened to the poor man? What about the dog?"

"Oh no, Aunt Gigi, we left Aggy all by herself there. We have to go back and get her," Derek's voice shook as he made this announcement.

"Don't worry boys, I thought about that already. I will pick her up and bring her to my house. Come by tomorrow and you can visit with her. She will be fine."

"Thank you, Aunt Gigi," both boys expressed their gratitude.

Aunt Gigi winked at the boys and headed out to her car to pick up the dog.

"Thank goodness you are both not hurt."

"Oh Mom, we're fine. It's Mr. Costa that's hurt. We can't figure out what happened to him and why he was out there."

"Yeah, Davey, but we're going to figure out this mystery, right Bro?"

"You bet, Derek, we will!"

"TT" was being shared and they were already working out the problem.

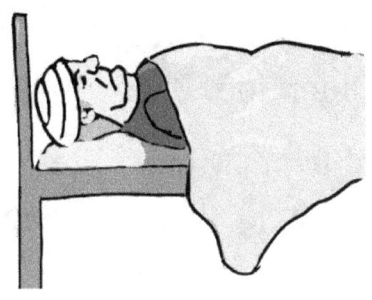

CHAPTER FIFTEEN

Visit with Aggy and Mr. Costa

"Hey boys, where are you going in such a hurry? You didn't finish your breakfast."

"We're not very hungry, Mom. Besides Aunt Gigi is waiting for us.

She has Aggy at her house and we want to see how she's doing."

"Okay, boys. Run on ahead but let me know how things are. Okay? I like to be in the loop too."

"No problem, Mom. We'll let you know," Derek agreed and Davey nodded.

"Hurry up slow poke! I'm going to beat you today for sure."

"Ha, I don't think so, Derek."

Davey raced on and barely edged out his brother but not for long. Derek was on a mission to see his favorite dog.

Derek jumped off his bike and ran up Aunt Gigi's steps just ahead of Davey who was not happy to say the least. He wasn't used to losing.

Aunt Gigi opened the door before Derek could knock wearing a wide smile. Behind her legs was a light brown no longer scraggly-looking dog.

"Wow, Aunt Gigi she looks so clean and not scraggly anymore," Derek chuckled with delight.

"She is so light colored now. I thought she was dark brown. She must have been pretty dirty," Davey added.

"Come on in, boys and meet Aggy. She is a lovely dog. We have been getting acquainted. Haven't we, girl?"

Aggy panted and patted Aunt Gigi's leg with her paw.

The boys looked on in awe at how friendly Aggy was and sat down next to her and patted and rubbed her all over. Aggy was delighted to make more new friends.

"Boys, I called the hospital and talked to the doctor on call when Mr. Costa was brought in. I told him a little fib that I was the patient's sister. Mr. Costa is awake now and doing well. It if wasn't for Aggy keeping him warm he may not have made it."

Turning to Aggy, Aunt Gigi said, "Thank you, dear Aggy, for saving your master."

The boys joined in and said, "Yeah, Aggy, you are a wonder dog. Thank you for helping us find him too."

"Now boys, how would you like to go visit Mr. Costa? I would like him to know that Aggy is being taken care of until he is well again to do it himself."

"Okay, sure. We have to ask Mom first though." Derek knew how his mother worried.

"No problem, I already called her before you arrived. She approved as long as I am with you."

The boys were out the door and waiting at Aunt Gigi's car. She grabbed her pocketbook and keys and yelled out to Uncle George to watch the dog.

Mr. Costa was lying in bed when they got there with his head wrapped in bandages and hooked up to an IV. He wasn't aware they were in the room until Aunt Gigi spoke his name.

"Oh, I didn't hear you come in. Are you the kind lady that found me?"

"Yes, I am Gigi and these boys are my great nephews, Davey and Derek. We were on an adventure to find the owner of a brown dog who came to my yard a couple of days ago. Your dog is a lovely creature, Mr. Costa. I wanted you to know that I am taking good care of her with the help of my great nephews here."

"Oh thank you so much! Yes, I am fortunate to have her. She must have been trying to get some help for me. I noticed a few days ago that she didn't have her collar on but looked everywhere in the house and around the yard. I know I can buy her another one but it was what was on her collar that was important to me. It was a locket engraved with my wife's name. I gave it to Agatha for our 50th anniversary. When she died I put it on the dog's collar and had it engraved with her name, Aggy, and my address and phone number in case she got lost."

"I was really lonely after my wife, Agatha, died two years ago. I went to the pound one day and brought this dog home with me. It was lucky for me that I did. I named her Aggy after my wife. Now when I called Aggy I feel as if my wife is close by."

"That's a beautiful story, Mr. Costa. Now do you remember what happened to you before you fell?" Aunt Gigi began the questioning.

"Please call me Henry. Well, I heard a noise in the backyard and went to investigate. Aggy rushed out ahead of me and started barking wildly. It was too dark to see what was out there.

Aggy growled and ran toward the trees. I couldn't see where she was going but I followed her just the same. When I got to the ravine I lost my footing and tumbled down and must have hit my head on the rock at the bottom. I don't remember a thing after that."

"Have the police been here to see you yet, Henry?"

"Yes, they came early this morning as soon as the doctor told them I was awake. I told them what I just told you."

"We were looking around your yard when we heard Aggy barking. We found a new grave and a short distance away we found a bloody piece of plaid cloth."

"Oh, yes the grave was for a poor rabbit that was left dead by a coyote or fox or something. When I found it I buried the poor thing. I don't know about the bloody cloth."

"Where are the clothes you were wearing yesterday, Henry?" Aunt Gigi asked.

"Over there in the locker. I wore a dark shirt not plaid though."

Aunt Gigi peeked into the locker and noted the dark shirt, not a match to the cloth found.

"Well, I don't want to keep you awake. You need to get your rest. Do you have any other family that I could call for you?"

"Yes, my son but the nurse already called him. He is on his way from

North Carolina. I don't plan to be going anywhere for a few days. Then he will take me home. I will get in touch with you about Aggy. Can you leave me your name and number?"

Gigi placed her name and number on a slip of paper next to Henry's phone.

"Thank you again, Gigi, for all you and your nephews have done for me. Give Aggy a hug for me and tell her I love her and miss her and that we will be together soon."

"That I will do, Henry. Now take care and get well. I will call tomorrow to check up on you, okay? Maybe I can talk to your son when he arrives."

"Yes, that would be good. I will give him your number. Thank you. Oh…Gigi, could you do me a favor? Can you go check on my house and see if everything is in order and lock the doors. I have a key hidden outside so I will be able to get back in later. I'm worried that maybe someone might try to break in and steal my wife's jewelry. Some of it is valuable."

"Oh, of course, Henry. I would be happy to do that for you."

Henry's eyes were closing as he turned over and fell asleep. The threesome slipped out of the room and headed home. There was a lot yet to do and more clues to find.

One thing Aunt Gigi had to do was get the blood sample she took from Aggy's paw to the police for evaluation. It could be the answer to some of the questions that were going around in her head.

CHAPTER SIXTEEN

Bloody Clue Saved

Davey and Derek couldn't wait to get back to Aunt Gigi's so that they could play with Aggy. They were excited to get acquainted.

Aggy looked out the front window and panted as she watched for any sign of the lady's car. She was enamored with this lady who bathed, fed and cared for her. She missed her master but knew that he was hurt and hoped she would see him again. But in the meantime she was enjoying the care of his lady and her delicious treats.

Aunt Gigi pulled into her drive and the boys jumped out to race up the stairs to her house. Uncle George opened the door and stood aside as the boys headed into the kitchen and living room before finding Aggy looking out the window at Aunt Gigi.

"Hi Aggy! How are you, girl? We went to see Henry at the hospital. He misses you and says that he will see you soon. Do you want to play?" Derek gave Aggy a hug for Henry as he requested and was rewarded with a sloppy kiss on the face.

"Yuck, wet dog kisses!" Derek complained but loved every minute of the attention he was getting. He had always wanted a dog of his own.

"Hey, Derek, don't hog her. I want to pet Aggy too!"

Aggy was enjoying all the attention too and gave Davey one of her wet kisses.

Aunt Gigi watched the boys and Aggy playing together. She went into the kitchen to make a call to the police to report the bloody cloth that she had found. She had put it in a plastic bag to protect it from the elements.

When the police chief came on the phone she explained what she had found and he said, "Thank you, Mrs. Cornbloom, for reporting this. I will send a car by to pick up the cloth and the blood sample and have them tested. It may belong to the intruder's from Mr. Costa's yard."

"Yes, I thought so too. That is why I didn't want it to go missing. I'm sorry I didn't give it to the police at that time. I forgot about it once I saw Mr. Costa."

"I see. Thank you. Aren't you the great aunt of the junior detectives, Davey and Derek Donato, who helped us on another case? Are they on a new case? The police chief inquired, amusement in his tone."

"Ha, yes I am their great aunt. And yes, they are on this case."

"I would appreciate being kept abreast of any other clues you or they may find on this case," Chief said as he chuckled.

"Of course Chief, we will be happy to help," Gigi giggled back.

"Well, thank you. Goodbye, Mrs. Cornbloom."

"Goodbye, Chief."

***

Barking could be heard from the living room and Aunt Gigi went to investigate.

"Well, are you three well acquainted yet?"

"Oh yes, we're best of friends now, Aunt Gigi," Derek replied with a beaming smile.

"I guess you could say that we are friends," Davey agreed with his own wide smile.

"Boys, I thought you would like to know that the police would appreciate your help on this case. They are coming by to pick up the bloody cloth sample for evaluation," Aunt Gigi said with a smile and a wink.

"Really, Aunt Gigi? That's awesome!" Derek jumped up with surprise.

"Wow, they need us, Davey! Would you believe that? We're getting well known! Ha!"

"When are the police going to know what type of blood the sample is and who it belongs to?"

"Well, I don't know but I'm sure they will keep in touch. We have some work ahead of us, boys. We are going back to Mr. Costa's house for a more thorough search. I have a feeling we may find something there. Are you ready?"

"Yeah, let's go, Aunt Gigi!" both boys exclaimed excitedly as Aggy joined in and barked.

After telling George to watch over Aggy once again Aunt Gigi grabbed the boys' hands and off they went by PT.

CHAPTER SEVENTEEN

Theft at Tangerine Lane

There was a kaleidoscope of swirling colors and a high pitched sound as the threesome traveled faster than ever through a tunnel. The twins closed their eyes and held their breath and clung tightly to Aunt Gigi's hands as they traveled.

This time they arrived on the front porch of Mr. Costa's house. Knowing from her previous visit that the front door was unlocked, Aunt Gigi easily opened it, wearing her black leather gloves, and invited the twins in.

"Stay right behind me boys. Don't touch anything or you could become suspects in this case."

"Oh, do you think the police would actually think we had something to do with Mr. Costa getting injured?" Derek was shocked.

"Well, yes if you leave your prints on anything. You automatically become a suspect. So please be diligent boys." Aunt Gigi was serious as she moved along stealthily.

The boys followed her lead and looked around as they passed each room. Aunt Gigi slowed down as she came to the bedrooms. There were two of them and she peeked into the first one but didn't go in. The next one she entered and stopped in front of the bureau which had drawers opened. There was a space free of dust in the center of the bureau.

Aunt Gigi leaned closer and noticed an earring that was sticking out of the doily by the lamp. She slipped it into a baggy and put it in her pocket.

Davey used "TT" to alert Derek.

Hey, Derek, did you see that. Aunt Gigi found an earring and put it into a baggy just like on the crime shows on TV.

Yeah, I noticed. Maybe she's working undercover for them? Ha!

Did you hear that?

What did you hear, Derek?

I heard a crunch like someone was walking around outside. We better tell Aunt Gigi. Could be the police.

"Aunt Gigi, Derek just heard someone outside. Maybe we should get out of here. It could be the police. What will they think if they find us here?"

"Did you now, boys? Okay, we are just about finished here. Watch where you are walking and follow in my footsteps again. We are going to do PT as you call it back to my house," Aunt Gigi chuckled at the boys' surprised looks.

"How did you know we call it that, Aunt Gigi?" Davey queried.

"Oh I have my ways, boys. I have my ways. I like the sound of it myself. You are good at acronyms, Derek."

"Thanks, Aunt Gigi!" Derek looked pleased with himself and appreciated the compliment especially from Aunt Gigi.

"Okay boys, take my hands and let's move out before we get into trouble with the police. They are outside looking around. I spotted them out the window as we entered the second bedroom."

The back door opened slowly and in walked two police officers as Aunt Gigi finished her spell and she and the twins disappeared in a swirl of colors and lights.

One officer blinked twice when he noticed colors floating around. He poked his fellow officer who looked at where he was pointing but the colors had disappeared.

"Did you see that Brian?"

"No, are you seeing ghosts now, Steve?"

"No but I did see something. I just don't know what it was." The officers walked away from this phenomenon and began their search of Mr. Costa's house.

As they moved toward the bedroom Brian stepped on something that crunched under foot. The officer picked up his foot and noticed a gemstone of a red color. He picked it up with a tweezer and placed it into a new baggy and zipped it shut.

They entered the bedroom where Aunt Gigi and the boys had just been and looked closely at the top of the bureau as Aunt Gigi had. He also noticed the dustless area where something must have been and was now missing. He made notes in his pad and did a thorough search of the rest of the house before calling into the station to report their findings.

***

Aunt Gigi and the twins arrived in the center of the living room much to the surprise of Aggy who was still looking out the window waiting for their return.

Aggy began barking and jumping up and down pleased to have them back again. The boys hugged and patted her and showed their delight too.

"Nice to see you too, Aggy. Yes, we missed you girl. Did George give you a treat while we were gone?"

Aggy wagged her tail and barked in reply.

"No, he didn't? Well, let's fix that, right boys?"

"Yeah, let's get some treats, Aggy!" both boys proclaimed.

Aunt Gigi pulled out her bag of tricks in the kitchen cabinet and in it were some doggy treats. She picked out a few and tossed them to the boys so they could give them to Aggy. Aggy was right next to them the second the treats were in the boys' hands. She wagged her tail and looked so sweet the boys couldn't help laugh as they in turn handed Aggy a delicious doggy treat.

Aggy wagged her tail more excitedly as she chomped on each treat. The boys caught what looked like a smile on her adorable face.

As the boys were busy with Aggy Aunt Gigi went into her bedroom and called the police to report what she had found at Mr. Costa's house. She reported that Mr. Costa asked her to check on his house to make sure everything was in order.

Upon hanging up the phone Aunt Gigi silently used her powers to lock both front and back doors of Mr. Costa's house once she knew the police were through with their investigation. Now Mr. Costa's house was safe from burglars because she had left a spell on the doors so that no one but Mr. Costa or his son could enter the house.

***

"Oh boys, would you like a snack now too? There is still plenty of time before dinner. I have some snacks that would make a great lunch. I am going to make a cup of tea for George and me and milk for you two."

"Yeah, sounds good to me, Aunt Gigi," Davey readily approved.

"Hmm, I could use something myself," Derek agreed.

"Oh Aunt Gigi, should we tell the police about what we found at Mr. Costa's house today?" Davey probed now on full stomach.

"Well, as a matter of fact, I already called them. It is all taken care of."

"I think we have to leave it in their hands. They have all the information that we have from Mr. Costa."

"I hope Mr. Costa gets better soon and can go home with his son. But what about Aggy? Will he be taking her away with him?"

"I guess we will find out soon. We have to let Mr. Costa get well first before bothering him. Okay, Derek?"

"Okay, I guess. But if he needs to find a home for Aggy, Davey and I can take him."

"What, Derek? What did you say? We can't do that! Mom would have a fit! She hasn't let us have a dog in our eleven years. What makes you think that she will now?"

"Oh, I think she will once she meets Aggy. Who wouldn't love her?" Derek looked at Aggy with much affection.

"What do you say, Aggy? Do you want to come home with Davey and me?"

Aggy knew something was being said about her and barked in agreement as her tail did a wide swish back and forth.

"Boys, why don't you ask your mother if she wouldn't mind having Aggy stay with you overnight first?"

"Okay, that would be a good way to do it. She may agree. Can you call her and put in a good word for Aggy too, Aunt Gigi?"

"I certainly will. Now it's time for you to get on home before it gets dark. Do you want me to drive you and you can come back tomorrow to pick up your bikes?"

"No, it's okay. We can get home quickly on our bikes. Besides I need to beat Derek home today."

"Oh no you don't Davey. Bye, Aunt Gigi. Thank you for everything today. See you tomorrow," Derek said and raced out the door ducking underneath Aunt Gigi's open arms.

Davey followed closely behind and did the same thing.

Aunt Gigi held onto Aggy as the boys' raced away. Aggy hung her head and looked sad to see them go.

Aunt Gigi patted Aggy's head and whispered, "Don't worry, girl. They'll be back soon."

CASE
CLOSED

CHAPTER EIGHTEEN

Case Closing

The twins raced home and arrived at
the same time. They discussed by
"TT" the findings of the case and
planned to sum things up on their
marker board.

"Hey boys, did you have a good time with Aunt Gigi today? Sounds like you had some excitement with the dog, huh?"

"Oh, did Aunt Gigi call you?" Derek asked hesitantly.

"Yes, she did. I know all about Aggy. When can I meet her?"

"Huh, what did you say, Mom?" Davey looked shocked by his Mom's statement.

Derek jumped up and hugged his mother with tears in his eyes. "Can we really have her visit for a little while?"

"Yes, I don't see why not," Laura smiled as her own tears threatened to fall.

Davey and Derek hugged each other and ran in circles not sure if this was a dream or not. They pinched one another to make sure.

"Ow, that hurt Davey!"

"Yeah, it did. But at least we know we are not dreaming, huh, Derek?"

The phone rang and Laura went to answer it leaving the boys going in circles and talking in their heads.

"Hello. Yes, this is Laura Donato. Yes, my sons are Davey and Derek Donato, junior detectives by their own design. Ha! Oh, I see. Just a moment."

"Boys, please come here. You have a phone call from the Chief of police."

"What, really? He wants to talk to us?"

"Well, that's what he said."

"Okay. Davey you talk to him first okay?"

Davey picked up the phone and listened for several minutes before answering. "Yes, sir. That is correct. Do you need us to go to the station? Oh, okay. You're welcome. Goodbye."

"Wait, Davey. Did he want to talk to me too?"

"No, he just needed us to verify what Aunt Gigi told them about what we found out in Mr. Costa's yard. He also thanked us for our assistance on another case. He sounded like he was laughing before he said goodbye."

"Really? Maybe he didn't believe us. Did the police finish their detective work already?"

"Well, they said they are on their way to solving it thanks to the work we and Aunt Gigi did."

"Wow that is really cool, Bro!"

"That was nice of the Chief to call though, boys. He didn't have to do that. I am proud of you both." Laura smiled and patted her boys on the heads.

"Yeah, I guess it was," Davey agreed.

The phone rang once again but this time it was Aunt Gigi. Laura picked it up and smiled as she heard her aunt's voice.

"Hi Aunt Gigi. Yes, we just heard from the police chief. He was pleased with the boys' help. Okay, sure. Do you want to talk to them? Just a minute."

"Derek and Davey, it's Aunt Gigi. Come over here and I will put her on speaker."

"Okay, Aunt Gigi, go ahead. You are on speaker so we can all hear you."

"Well, I just got off the phone with the police chief. He called to thank us for our help on this case. Also, he said they found the man from the blood sample we gave him. He was in the system and had been arrested in the past for theft."

"Did they find the jewelry that he stole from Mr. Costa's house?" Derek asked hoping to hear positively on this.

"Yes, the man pawned the jewels and the pawn shop reported this fact once they were alerted to look for this jewelry."

"But what about the locket that was on Aggy's collar?"

"Yes, that was there too. The man admitted to being guilty of taking it and frightening Mr. Costa that night he fell. He also said he was sorry that Mr. Costa was hurt. He didn't realize how serious his injuries were. He ran away because he feared being arrested for his past and present regressions."

"Aunt Gigi, how did this man know about Mrs. Costa's jewels?"

"He said that he saw the dog with the gold locket on her collar one day when he was driving by. It caught his eye and he came back a number of times and tried to get a closer look at the locket. One day he managed to stop the dog and looked at it closely. The address was engraved on the back of the locket as Mr. Costa had told us. He grabbed the locket off of Aggy's neck that day. He came back another night to look for more jewels. He waited for Mr. Costa to come out to investigate what Aggy was barking about. The man went into the house once Mr. Costa fell down the ravine and got away with the jewelry."

"Oh boy, he is in trouble. So that piece of material was from this man's shirt with his blood. How did he get blood on his shirt?"

"Oh you are a true detective, Derek." Aunt Gigi laughed.

"Aggy bit the man on his arm and ripped his shirt. Some of the blood dropped on Aggy's paw. That is what we saw when we first found her. It was the man's blood."

"Oh, I see. It all makes sense now, Aunt Gigi," Davey surmised happily.

"Well, I am glad that this case is over but it isn't over for Mr. Costa and Aggy. What's going to happen to them?"

"It's funny you ask. Mr. Costa's son called me right after the police chief. He is taking his father back home with him to live. Unfortunately he cannot have a dog where he lives. Mr. Costa needs to find someone to take care of Aggy. Do you know someone who might be able to do that?"

"Oh yes, we do! Mom, can we take Aggy? Please! Please!" the twins both pleaded.

Aunt Gigi waited for Laura to answer before ringing the doorbell.

As soon as she heard 'yes' she pressed the bell and stood holding Aggy by her side.

"Oh, Aunt Gigi. I need to answer the door. Hold on a minute."

"Laura, it's only me. We can hang up now and talk in person."

The twins raced ahead to the door and pulled it open. Standing there much to their delight were Aunt Gigi, Uncle George and Aggy.

Before Laura could invite them all in the boys grabbed hold of Aggy and hugged her tight. Aggy was happy too because she provided wet sloppy kisses on both of the boys' faces.

"Boys, please let Aunt Gigi and Uncle George come in."

"Oh sorry Aunt Gigi and Uncle George. Please come in," both boys announced still possessively holding onto Aggy.

"Well, I take it that you are agreeable to having a dog in your home, Laura?" Aunt Gigi inquired.

"Oh, how can I say no to these boys? They have been good boys and I know they have always wanted a dog. I think they are old enough to take on this responsibility."

With all the barking and noise Donald, the twins' father, came into the kitchen to see what was going on. He had fallen asleep watching TV but all the noise had woken him up.

"Hi Aunt Gigi, Uncle George, what's going on out here? Whose dog is this? Hey fella, how are you?"

"Sorry Dad, he's a she, and she's ours!" both boys announced.

"Really? Laura, you said yes to this?" Donald winked at her.

"Well, it's about time, huh boys?"

Donald sat on the floor and joined the boys as they patted and played with Aggy.

The phone rang once again. This time Laura announced it was a Mr. Costa and he wanted to speak with the boys.

Davey and Derek grabbed the phone and put it on speaker once again before saying, "Hello, Mr. Costa. Thank you for letting us take care of Aggy."

"Oh it is my pleasure and Aggy's too I am sure. I hope that I can come by later to visit with her before I leave with my son. Maybe you and your family can come down to North

Carolina for vacation sometime and bring Aggy for a visit."

"Oh yes, we would love to do that. Thank you again, Mr. Costa," Davey and Derek said together.

"How are you feeling now, Henry?" Aunt Gigi asked.

"Oh, is that you Gigi? I'm doing much better, thank you. We will be leaving in a couple of days. I hope to see you too before I go. You and your husband are welcome to come visit me along with the twins and their family."

"Oh thank you, Henry. I think I would like that and so would George."

"Well, thank you all again. I don't know what would have happened if you hadn't come to find me," Henry's voiced choked up.

"Now, don't even think about it, Henry. We are pleased to help and so happy that everything turned out well for you. Did you hear from the police?"

"Yes, they told me they picked up the guy and got Agatha's jewelry too. I want you to have some of it, Gigi. Of course I want to give Aggy her locket back too."

"Oh, no Henry, I can't take anything of Agatha's. Please keep it and give it to your family. Thank you though for your kindness and generosity. Take care. Look forward to seeing you soon."

"Okay, Gigi. Thank you. Look forward to seeing you all too. Give Aggy a hug for me until I can give her one myself."

"Will do, Mr. Costa," the boys declared.

"Goodbye everyone," Mr. Costa ended the call.

CHAPTER NINETEEN

A Sad Goodbye

The twins were ecstatic to add Aggy to their family. It had been a few days since Aggy had come to stay with them. They played outside, inside and everywhere in the house driving their mother crazy. They were underfoot wherever she happened to be.

"Boys, please go outside or up to your room. I am trying to clean the house. You are in my way," Laura smiled through her scolding.

"Okay, Mom. Let's go, Aggy! We'll take her for a walk, okay?" Derek attached Aggy's leash as the boys led the dog out the back door.

***

A dark sedan pulled up and a man got out and leaned in to help an older man out of the car. They walked up the path to the front door and rang the bell.

Aggy suddenly stopped running around and headed to the front of the house with the boys in tow. She began barking excitedly and ran up to the two men standing on the front stoop.

"Aggy, how are you girl?" the older man exclaimed as he bent down carefully and rubbed her head.

The boys came up behind Aggy and were surprised to see Mr. Costa petting Aggy. He was looking a little pale but at least he was walking on his own.

"Hi Mr. Costa," Davey said with a wide smile as he reached out and shook the man's hand.

"Hey, Davey and Derek. How are you doing with Aggy? Is she behaving herself?"

"Oh she sure is, Mr. Costa!" Derek announced as he patted Aggy on her back and then reached forward to shake Mr. Costa's hand too.

Laura stood at the front door and waited for the boys to allow Mr. Costa to move into the house.

"Hi, Mr. Costa, I presume. Please come in. I am Laura Donato, Davey's and Derek's mother. It's so nice to finally meet you. I have heard a lot about what happened. I hope you are doing better now."

"Yes, I am doing much better, thank you, Laura. Oh, this is my son, Richard."

Richard shook Laura's hand as she led them into the kitchen. She pulled out a chair for Mr. Costa and Richard. Laura busied herself putting on a pot of coffee and pulled out some cake from the freezer to warm up.

"Please have a seat while I prepare some coffee and cake. My husband is not home yet but is expected shortly."

"Please don't go to any trouble. We are only stopping by for a few minutes to visit with you and say goodbye to Aggy," he said as he looked over at the dog with a sad look in his eyes.

"Aggy is a sweet dog. The boys love her already. They will take good care of her I will make sure."

"Thank you, I'm sure they will, Laura. Aggy and I have been close since I lost my wife. She took Agatha's place in my heart and kept me going. But now it is time for her to have some younger masters to care for her. I may not have much time left. I hope you and your family will come and visit me and bring Gigi and George too. She is a lovely lady and I owe both her and your boys my life." Mr. Costa's face was ashen and tears formed in his tired eyes.

"We will try to do that, Mr. Costa."

"Richard, write down your address and phone number so that they can contact us when they can come to visit."

Richard did as he was told but his face showed sadness and pain from something he was holding back.

Laura leaned over and took the paper with the information and patted Richard's shoulder as she passed by. She made eye contact with him and his eyes told her more than she wanted to know. Mr. Costa did not have much time left. He was sicker than he led on.

They all sat quietly drinking coffee and eating chocolate cake as the boys and Aggy ran around the kitchen chasing each other.

Mr. Costa smiled and said, "It's so good to see Aggy happy and active. I have not been well nor young enough to run around with her like that."

Laura nodded in understanding and replied, "I think Aggy will miss you, Mr. Costa."

"Yes, she will for a little while," he sighed.

"Dad, I think we should get on the road now. Our flight leaves in an hour and a half."

"Okay, Rich. Let's go," Mr. Costa turned toward the boys and Aggy and announced, "well it's time to say goodbye, girl."

Aggy knew something was happening and she turned toward her master and gave him sloppy wet kisses all over his face and hands and laid her head against his legs.

"Goodbye boys, take care of Aggy and have fun. She needs you. Maybe we will see each other again soon."

Richard took his father's arm and guided him up out of the chair.

"Bye, Mr. Costa, thank you again for letting us take Aggy. We promise to take good care of her."

"I know you will."

Laura leaned in and gave Mr. Costa a hug. She shook Richard's hand and whispered in his ear then said aloud,

"Have a safe trip. We'll talk to you soon."

Laura walked the men out to their car and she and the boys waved their goodbyes as Aggy barked a goodbye.

"Hey Mom, what did you whisper to Mr. Costa's son?" Davey asked inquisitively.

"I said I was sorry that his dad wasn't doing well and told him to keep in touch."

"How do you know Mr. Costa isn't doing well? He looked okay. He's just old." Derek queried.

"Just say that it's a mother's intuition. Okay?"

Derek was already running after Aggy and didn't hear his mother's response.

He had more important things to do – have fun with Aggy.

Davey watched his mother's face as she walked back into the house. He knew what she meant. Mr. Costa was going to die soon. This thought made him sad that he wouldn't see Mr. Costa again. He would do his best to help his brother take care of Aggy – a special gift from Mr. Costa.

Another case was solved and the boys now had a dog. Davey used "TT" to discuss their relief over having the successful outcome of another case.

Well, Bro, we did it again! Another case completed and look what we got out of this case – a dog! Pretty cool!

Yes Derek, pretty cool! Thanks to Mr. Costa, that is.

Racing up the street was Cat. His face was flushed as he jumped off his bike and ran over to see the boys and their dog.

"Hey, guys, all is good with the case, huh?"

"Yep, all is good, Cat. Come meet Aggy."

Aggy jumped up to give Cat a welcome with a big sloppy wet kiss.

"Yuck, she gives sloppy wet kisses! We're going to have to introduce Aggy to Elmer. He's going to love her!"

"I bet he will!" the twins exclaimed through chuckles.

THE END

A NOTE FROM THE AUTHOR

Thank you for purchasing one of Jemsbooks. If you like this book, a review would be greatly appreciated wherever you purchased it. Please go to my website for more children's books: http://www.jemsbooks.com.

My goal is to encourage children of all ages to read. Parents, please read to your children daily when they are young to help instill a love of reading into their lives.

When I write children's stories I try to make them gentle without anything that would frighten young children. My themes deal in life lessons and teaching young children how to be polite, kind and sensitive to others' feelings. I want children to know that it is okay to be different. It is extremely important that all children feel safe and loved in their homes and in their lives.

These stories are mainly to entertain, delight and teach children about life lessons and for the sheer joy of reading. I hope your children will enjoy these magical stories and learn valuable lessons that will stay with them for a lifetime.

Reading Gives You Wings to Fly!
Soar with Jemsbooks!

With Blessings & Love,

Janice Spina

ABOUT THE AUTHOR

Janice Spina is a retired administrative secretary from a school system in Massachusetts. She has always loved writing poetry and children's stories.

This is the fourth book in this middle-grade series. Janice has published eight children's books for Preschool-Grade 3. She has also published two novels under J.E. Spina. She continues to write more children's books and is in the process of editing more books for publication.

Look for more Jemsbooks on her website

http://www.jemsbooks.com

Amazon Author Page for all
Jemsbooks:
http://amazon.com/author/janicespina7

Barnes & Noble:
http://www.barnesandnoble.com/s/Jani
ce+Spina/_/N-
8q8?_requestid=1181730

Follow her on:

Twitter: http://twitter.com/janice_spina

Facebook Main Page:
http://www.facebook.com/janice.spina.
9

FB Author Page:
http//www.facebook.com/janicespina7

FB Novelist Page:
http://www.facebook.com/jespina77

LinkedIn:
http://www.linkedin.com/pub/janice-
spina/59/321/a01/

She also has a blog
http://www.jemsbooks.wordpress.com

She reviews books and talks about her adventures in writing and publishing, travels, and authors' guest posts and interviews.

Janice lives in New Hampshire with her husband, John, who is her illustrator and cover creator.

Janice's slogan is: ***Reading Gives You Wings to Fly!***

ABOUT THE ILLUSTRATOR

Dr. John Spina is a retired elementary and middle school principal from a school system in Massachusetts.

John has illustrated and created covers for eight children's books for PS-Grade 3. This is the fourth book in this middle-grade series he has illustrated. He also created the covers for Janice's two novels, *Hunting Mariah* and *How Far Is Heaven* which she wrote under J.E. Spina.

He is currently working on illustrating more of Janice's books and covers.

Their joint goal is to encourage children of all ages to read.

www.ingramcontent.com/pod-product-compliance
Lightning Source LLC
Chambersburg PA
CBHW071155260626
47162CB00003B/1056